# The Cure For ADHD

## by Josh Davis

**Copyright © 2018 by Josh Davis**

All rights reserved. No part of this publication may be reproduced, distributed, or transmitted in any form or by any means, including photocopying, recording, or other electronic or mechanical methods, without the prior written permission of the publisher, except in the case of brief quotations embodied in critical reviews and certain other noncommercial uses permitted by copyright law.

This is a work of fiction

# TABLE OF CONTENTS

| | |
|---|---|
| **A Helluva Morning** | **4** |
| **Light My Fire** | **8** |
| **I Tailored the Devil: A Brief Conversation with Satan** | **19** |
| **On Edge** | **33** |
| **Fender Bender** | **52** |
| **Remember, Satan Loves You** | **130** |
| **ABOUT THE ARTIST** | **168** |

# A Helluva Morning

The sun exploded through dust stained, white drapes in a frenzied ray of gleaming light. Jill's closed eyelids heated to a dull throb of pain, waking her once resting mind. She raised her arm to her face with instinctual reflex; the glare was too bright. Her eyes flickered open and shut like a loading computer booting up the day's programs. Her vision honed in quickly, sending the blurriness away in a projection-like demise.

At the instant her vision honed, she noticed her son standing at the foot of her bed. His face held a look of confused calm that almost resembled guilt in a childlike way. Once again, the brightness overtook her vision in a fierce storm of glow. She shoved her hand into the air, giving an invisible high-five to shield her squinted eyes. It worked only partially, her son still visible at the edge of the hand – silhouetted with flash.

"Zachery? Are you okay?"

The boy winced as if being startled awake.

His eyes, once fixed below his mother, now met hers with tremendous concentration.

"Mom. Heaven is burning. It was finally defeated." The words came out of him with an eerie ease. The gracefulness of his tone was as normal spoken as "the sky is blue". Only, Jill had a feeling the sky was not blue today. She felt truth behind her son's insane statement.

"Honey, what are you talking about?" She launched out of bed quicker than she had intended, tripping herself to her knees before her son. Out of adrenalized concern she grabbed his shoulders.

"What's going on? What happened?" The questions came out desperate. Zachery met her eyes once more. His face transformed into that of an older being, with a maniacal grin she had never seen before. It was the face of inconceivable evil. He stretched his mouth open, propelling a heinous laughter that echoed through the house with enormous reverberation.

Jill hurriedly crawled to her bedroom window on one elbow, grabbing the bottom of the drapes and ripping them open. The sky was not blue. In fact, the sky was not there at all. A gargantuan fireball filled the above in a roaring wind of chaos. Strains of fire and smoke streamed down like a catastrophic volcano eruption. People stood outside their houses in a dumbfounded gaze, watching Armageddon erupt and engulf them.

Zachery's laughter rang in her ears in a shrill, deafening tone. She turned back slowly to her son. His eyes, nose, and mouth flowed with blood as his chuckling turned into a gurgled giggle. As madness began to enter Jill, he stopped at once with an incoherent gaze. Fresh blood dripped consistently from his face to the hardwood floor. His lifeless eyes looked to nowhere as he began speaking softly under his breath.

"All damned, all damned, all damned..." he repeated to himself, each time getting louder than the last until once again he was screaming with a worn out voice. Jill blacked out with one last rational thought inside her perplexed and panicked mind: *Is this real?*

Her maddening demeanor let loose its firm grip as she looked around frantically, covered in splattered brain and blood. She found herself blank gazed and crouched above her now headless son, his once small cranium a mashed mess beneath her. She looked to her hands to see a bible in her possession – the Old Testament hardback her grandma had given her. She had bashed her son's brains in with a tool normally used to bring hope. The gold rimmed cross on the cover (now stained with red around the rim) shined glaringly into her sensitive eyes.

    Jill lowered her head and began to laugh hysterically.

# Light My Fire

The stars were barely visible in the dark abyss of night. Peter and Robin's conversation topics seemed to be depleting rapidly, until finally they fell silent on each other. The black Monte Carlo sat alone in the darkness, beside the Birmingham Cliffs, where they thought they could stargaze. But not on this night of ominous gloom. Nothing much to see, except a few stragglers amongst the dreary canvas in the sky. And now, 'silent' conversation was resorted to. Peter adjusted his Letterman Jacket and cleared his throat.

"So, I guess we gotta figure out something to do," Robin said, smirking and clearing her throat, as if completing a ceremonial task before speaking.

"Yeah, I guess we do. All the stars are hiding on us." Peter clicked on the headlights, which were vastly consumed by the night, the silence somehow making the air darker.

Peter jutted a long finger to the blackness.

"This is one of the darkest nights I've ever seen."

Images of mysterious creatures (or humans for that matter) flooded across the forefront of her mind. Hiding in the night, easily unseen. Fuck, Sasquatch could open her door and it'd already be too late. *The fog of darkness*, Robin thought, getting chills. This was her first date with Peter, and the anxiety of that, mixed with the lack of visibility, created lumps in her dry throat.

"How about we head someplace more... lit?" Robin implemented nervously. "This black is making me... uneasy."

Peter smiled down to her, like an adult would an irrational child. "This could be the perfect chance to get to know each other."

As hesitant as Robin was, she partially agreed, with a bit of shake in her voice. "Okay, but not for too much longer." She really liked Peter and wanted to see where he could take her; besides being one of the most popular guys in school, he was cute in a "prince-dream-like kind of way". Instead of a risk taker, Robin had always been the cautious type. But with only two weeks left 'til graduation, it was time to be a little more adventurous.

Peter smiled, warmer than before, setting her more at ease. "How about we ask each other some deeper questions, to, I don't know… get a little more personal, closer?" His face changed as he asked, waiting apprehensively for a reply to a question he wasn't sure he should be asking.

"Okay. Like, what kind?" Robin immediately asked, now feeling bolder than ever.

Peter looked pleased with her reply and she was relieved, not wanting to screw up a 'good thing' with him.

"Are you a virgin?" he asked, suddenly and forcefully as if he couldn't stop the words from vomiting forth. He turned his head to his window as if ashamed. Robin thought of his bashfulness as cute, giving her more ambition to reply.

"To be completely honest," her breath grew heavy, not fully realizing her panic, "no, I am not." The words came bursting out before she could give it much more thought and coward out with a lie. The answer seemed to please Peter, his face glowing as the moon made an appearance and shone inside.

"Cool, me either," Peter said in a nothing-to-be-ashamed-of tone. "I lost mine when I was sixteen," he added. Robin knew immediately the next question to be asked. What age had she been? But what would be her answer? The truth? She was fourteen when her innocence was lost, a young age, and she dare not say an age younger than his.

"Me too, sixteen." She knew the lie was clearly evident on her face, but she didn't care. She felt a deep urge to match Peter's bluntness, without revealing too much.

"Well, I- I guess it's your turn." Peter said as he lost his smile, becoming more subtle.

Robin thought it over quickly, already knowing her question.

"What are your intentions towards me?" The subtlety in his face evolved to a look of concentration, as if preparing for a long and important speech. He looked to his lap.

"I had this dream." His voice was stern and focused. "In this dream, there was an angel. Nothing I could've ever believed I was seeing. She was absolutely *beautiful*." Peter emphasized the "beautiful" to make his point stick through. "I was trying to reach her, trying to grab her hand, but she kept slipping away." His eyes glistened with intensity.

Robin had no clue where this story was going, but in a way, she anticipated the punchline, the root to where this story would sink.

"She was engulfed in these..." Peter outstretched his arms and waved them around himself, "these gorgeous, bright flames. I can always feel the heat seep into me, igniting my spirit."

Robin's own curiosity got the better of her, anxiously spitting out her next words. "What does this all have to do with me?" Peter flinched at the interruption and quickly answered.

"You look just like her."

His words set her back, almost aweing her to a vegetable state. Her nerves warmed inside her body, she was pleasantly graced.

"I look like her, huh?" She used sarcasm to hide her awkwardness, though it was fruitless. The girl was in fact impressed, but the guard could never be let down, not for a moment. "So, this dream gave you the courage to ask me out?" A slight but not unnoticed blush filled her cheeks. Peter chuckled at the question and just as frank, his face fell focused.

"I have to find my angel. I HAVE to; it's all that I have." Robin could have sworn she saw tears well up in his eyes. So much emotion has to conclude honesty, right?

"Well, we should take it slow, see where it takes us." She steadied her eyes on him, tucking her hair behind her ear. Peter flinched again at this statement, only now, his eyes frosted over with coldness. His face turned menacing.

"No, I must find out tonight. You have to be her." The caliber of his tone changed. It was demanding and forceful. Robin knew it immediately; the sinking feeling she felt, the crazed look in his eye, but nothing could have prepared her for what was to come.

"Yeah, well…" She tried to mask her uneasiness as best she could. "I don't really know what that means." Without thought, she reached for her seatbelt, but neglected to fasten it.

"I didn't mean to confuse you, in fact, I'm kinda confused myself." The features in his soft complexion became heavy. It reminded Robin of a child, knowing they're guilty, but unwilling to resist temptation.

"I like you a lot. I think, maybe, you are the one I've been looking for all along," Peter said with a frightening depth in his eyes.

As much as Robin enjoyed the attention Peter was giving her, it was getting too heavy, too fast. The uncomfortability toll had reached its limit, and Robin wanted to go home.

"I'm sure we will see if it is what we both are looking for, but tonight, let's ease things up a bit."

She hoped she sounded as convincing as it felt. Hoping not to show her nervous meter, which had reached its boiling point.

Peter looked emotionally exhausted with disappointment. She noticed him making revolutionary decisions in his mind, what she did not know was his mind had already been made up.

"So, does the seatbelt mean you wish to go home?" Peter said as his left eyebrow rose drastically. It put a genuine smile on her face, lessening her eagerness. *He could just be a hopeless romantic, they could still exist, ya know?* The thought made her smile wider. She looked at the time.

"It is getting late, almost midnight," Robin said lowly.

Peter slowly reached down to the left side of his seat. The splash hit her face so abruptly, with a blasting sting. She gulped for breath but only burnt her lungs trying. The smell filled her nostrils with fumes, causing her to choke and cough. The liquid seeped into her eyes, blurring her vision. She tried once more to breathe, only, doing so caused more fumes to enter her lungs. Laughter erupted beside her. She barely acknowledged the sound of the car door opening. She began madly searching for the door handle. Cold tears poured from her burning, bloodshot eyes. Before she was able to grip the handle, her door flew open violently.

"I'm sorry, Robin, this has to be done. Baby, you are my destiny, to be set free." His voice was sincere and icy cold.

Robin's sight remained foggy. Peter only appeared to be a black figure.

"What did you throw all over me?" Her voice was harsh, broken, and crackly.

"Lighter fluid, I'm going to burn you, bitch." Bellowing laughter followed. He sounded as though he was joking around with his high school buddies.

His laughter ceased within seconds, frozen in place. His face morphed to pure dread. The tears caused by laughing, now flowed with misery and sorrow.

"It's driving me mad!" Peter screamed before collapsing to his knees, bawling. "I have to do it. I'm, I'm…" the crying overtook his words. "I'm obsessed!"

With her vision clear enough to attempt an escape, Robin waiting no longer, jolted upright, and as fast as she could, she sprinted away.

The cries turned once more to lunacy and he began after her.

Panic drove Robin's legs faster and faster. Getting away was her only shot at survival, she knew this.

Running forward, Peter reached into his jeans pocket, pulling out a shiny Zippo lighter. In a few more seconds, he'd be within tossing distance. And, as if God came down to help assist an angel in the making, Robin tripped over a shattered tree stump, landing heavily on her chest. Groaning, she quickly flipped onto her back, her ears ringing with a power as forceful as ten thousand jet engines.

Peter stood straight with his head down, tears staining his face, heavily panting, towering over her.

"It is you. I know it." Peter flicked the zippo open, struck the wheel and tossed it forward. The flame raged across Robin's chest first, instantly sticking her blouse to her bubbling skin. The shrill of her screams gargled out as the fire tore through her throat and exploded her larynx. Her hair melted simultaneously with her face, and her eye sockets oozed like a morbid wax figure on a low budget film.

And for that split moment, before the deterioration of Robin's face, Peter saw his 'Angel of Flame'. It was everything he had hoped it would be, and more. The love he felt in his dream was muffled compared to the beautiful aspect of reality.

But with the marvels of reality, also come the horrors. Robin burned for six minutes. The black, smoldering corpse was no longer Peter's angel. That blissful, short lived love scattered away into a mere memory.

He sank to the ground, taking her in his arms, and wept.

"I will find you again. Whatever it takes, I will find a way to keep you!" The heat of the steaming cadaver rose up to flush his sensitive skin. The charcoal surface of her body left his face blackened. Chunks of flesh stuck to his light blue jacket. What was left of her right breast had slipped down into her lap.

"You were so beautiful." His crying ceased like a clock striking its chord. He looked up from her empty sockets.

"I will find you again."

# I Tailored the Devil: A Brief Conversation with Satan

Humanity, in a certain point of view, is actually terrifying. To ponder one's existence, is to ponder the existence of life in general. But if one sees the truth that lies behind everyone's eyes, existence and humanity become a little clearer.

I was barely out of my teens, just entered manhood when I encountered Satan. I think maybe, that was a good thing. I was able to live the rest of my life from a different point of view. A point of view where everything is indeed right and wrong. A world where we as a human species have choices to make in life.

I can remember, as a child, having dreams of Heaven. I dreamt of tall, pearly gates that led to the 'Holy Land'. In front of the gates stood a line of people, or as one might think, people's souls. They stand in line to be judged accordingly, only, all their faces looked optimistic. The truth of the matter is, in terms of entering the 'Holy Land', we are all fucked. I've seen the evil that resides in every corner of the earth. I've felt the true sensation of being damned. As an older man in life now, it is quite frightening to realize how long it actually has been since my blindfold to the world had been slipped off.

When I did meet Him, his charm brought more fright than it did relief. He acted and looked as a man, but the power within him could be felt for miles.

I was working as a tailor's assistant in the town of Breckenview, Ohio. It was a quaint town, mostly country and well-mannered citizens – peaceful. It was a good time in my life; I still had hope for the future. It was as if that day I was still a child, but by nightfall I became an adult; knowing the truth of the universe was not an advantage.

It was a curse.

I remember the day like it was yesterday. It was the middle of July and the town had just gotten through the festivities of Independence Day. The sidewalks in town remained jam packed with loitering tourists. I was staying with my Uncle Murdoch, just on the outskirts of Breckenview for the summer. The relationship with my parents became a bitter contest of wills, and the only option I deemed fit was to move far away. A bold choice on my part but being the age of twenty-three, I had no reason to stay near their constant hovering, nagging natures.

I had just come in from outside, the blazing sun causing my skin to break out in a sticky, oily sweat. Mr. Rassenberg was in the back, making some final touches to a variety of expensive suits, reserved for a political dinner party for the week to follow. I can recall every detail about this day; it forever burnt a film reel in my mind. A sudden nauseous sensation washed over me mere minutes before He walked in. My knees trembled with a rush of exhaustion; somehow I felt thinner, smaller. Little did I know, the next customer to cross the threshold that scorching day was going to change my life.

It was around 2:30 pm when a shadow from the left began its creeping approach. The shadow seemed to engulf everything in its path; it consumed the sidewalk as it spread out. At one point it seemed unnaturally large, and for a fleeting second, it covered the sun's rays like fresh black tar covers pavement. The whole shop appeared to have been swallowed up, an eerie, shadowy hand slithering toward the shop's knob. The sharp ding of the doorbell snapped my peripheral vision back into retrospect. The shop was no longer in a death grip of darkness.

In walked a tall, slim man. His face was anything but menacing, and the overall vibe he immediately emanated was not that of fear, but quite the opposite. His jet black hair was slicked back tightly against his scalp. He wore a faded grey suit that looked used and battered, but still somehow held a hint of elegance. He closed the door slowly behind him with a welcoming smile spread across his face.

"Well, hello there, young man. I assume you are enjoying this rather lovely summer day?" The smile he bore grew even wider. I knew he wasn't from around the area. Breckenview locals are quick to spot an 'out of town' face. I, for one, had never seen this man. I would have surely remembered that smile, a smile that bred questions all on its own.

"Hi, sir, what can we do for you today?" I asked as I searched the back for Mr. Rassenberg, who was not at all interrupted from his work. I, to this day, do not even know if Mr. Rassenberg had seen or heard Him, or *could* see Him. On the contrary, it appeared he was oblivious to the gentleman's presence altogether. But that theory suggests the intention of His visit was specifically for me, which brings a new level of problems to the table.

He had a certain purpose to Him that I did not notice at the time. It was a look of meaning and explanation, an ancient knowledge no one else possessed, but yet, He acted calm and collected. He kept that smile and outstretched his bony hand.

"I'm new to town, and I'm afraid I am in need of a rather decent suit." His eyes gave a believable performance whilst concealing something dark that briefly flickered behind his pupils. The white around those eyes were glossy and becoming thin. "What's your name, son?" He added quickly.

The room all at once seemed too small for the two of us, making it hard to concentrate. It felt as though we were the only ones that existed in that exact moment. It was a terrifying feeling of the absolute power. I answered with a shaky voice, "Randy, sir. What kind of suit are we looking for today?" As I grabbed his rather large hand, a flicker of flame danced in both his pupils; this was not a hallucination. The flames whirled around his eyes like wind through trees, he blinked hard, and the ignited orange vanished.

"Well, what would you suggest? You see, I've been out of the swing of things for a while around here. I'm afraid I have yet to adapt to the new changes of the world. What would you refer for a man of my tall stature?" All the while his smile never once faltering, eye contact not for one moment disconnecting. The uncomfortability level that sparked between us forced me to back up suddenly. His face brightened from the obvious wince.

"We have some of our best suits right over here. Come take a look and see what best fits you." I walked with a fast pace over to the premier closet we usually use for the upper class customers. Mr. Rassenberg never once strayed from his work in the back.

The towering man followed closely, his smile reduced to a smirk, his long, pointed nose crunched up to a slight sneer. "Fabulous," He said in a sarcastic tone. I felt as though this encounter would never end, yet I could not put a finger on what was just not right with him. It was as if the atmosphere changed, grew cold and dry. I reached in, grabbed a brand new Russell Lonze suit from the rack and hurriedly held it up in front of myself.

"This has been the most commonly purchased this year. It is reviewed to also be the most popular choice for both luxury as well as comfort."

He looked the suit up and down and sneered around at me from behind. "It is too light. I'm going for black. I desire it to be the darkest of black possible. Kind of like life." He snickered, his nose crinkling back up and *that* smile returned, wider than ever. "Say? You wouldn't be frightened, would you?" His teeth were black around the gums, something I never noticed before. "You seem terribly nervous; surely I'm not the cause?"

I panicked from the unexpected question and answered abruptly. "Of course not, we have dark suits this way, sir." I ventured further into the vast closet with the strange man tight on my heels. I could now see that his eyes did not catch light, they were pitch black holes. The veins on his face darkened as his skin lightened to a pasty white. I grabbed the nearest black suit to my left. "This one should be perfect, tall size and the darkest of blacks we have." I once again held up the suit in front of me. His face was dull and indecisive as he stared at the suit without blinking.

"I think that may suffice, young man. Shall I get fitted?" He grabbed the suit from my hand and walked out of the closet; it was pure relief to have distance from him. His presence was heavy and exhausting.

I was about out of the closet, pulling the door shut, when I felt his breath hot on the back of my neck. I whipped around quickly to find him inches away. "Don't be frightened. You have noticed enough already, I suppose. No need in hiding anymore. I come with no threat, to you anyway," He said with a soft chuckle. "I hide, not because I am scared, only because mortals could not fathom the notion of my existence. They go to their churches to praise, to help them protect themselves from me, only not the danger. The danger is themselves."

He took a couple steps back, still glaring. My breath was short and my heart raced in my chest. "I am the Prince of the Unholy, the Wrath of the

Damned, I come only in passing. I have bigger dealings than scaring a young man today." He handed the suit back to me and stood calmly.

I could not muster any words. I tried to regain the breath that hitched in my throat and couldn't. Finally, with much guided pushing, I was able to utter a response. "I-I don't know what you are talking about, sir. But if you would like to try that suit on, our dressing rooms are right behind you." I figured acting ignorant to anything he said was an intelligent idea, but it only fed His appetite for conversation.

"The suit can wait." He placed his hands in the air in a polite halting fashion before he continued. "I would like to give you a gift of knowledge I have never dealt out before. It seems as though your thoughts are fixated on your parents. You're bitter inside, the world seems like a dark place to you. Family, friends, everybody, they are all strangers to you. The pain you feel is normal. I am comforted to know you never prayed to Him. Non-believer? No, I think not. You have anger towards Him; I feel it flowing from you. I know this because I have felt this same anger. The strong sense of abandonment you wield, you are absolutely right. You are all abandoned, you all are. God works in mysterious ways to cater to Himself. He doesn't bother Himself with your problems, so why should you bother yourself with His?" He reached his skinny fingers towards me quickly, placing his hand atop my head.

Images flash flooded through my mind like a raging storm; a soldier in armor knelt around a gust of roaring flames, his dirtied face tear streaked. The distressed soldier picked up his sword and screamed to the sky, the voice muffled yet not entirely incoherent. The fire soared around his body, igniting his flesh as bright, white wings burst from the soldier's back.

"I fought for Him; I gave my life for Him. Betrayal was not introduced by Judas, betrayal was introduced by God himself. He left me to burn in the underworld, to rot for the pride I held for my people." The man's voice amplified over the images. "I was not only a soldier in His army, we were brothers in arms. I lived my life by His code, until I realized the potential in myself that was being held back. It is always about power, even for gods. Once they cannot control you, they condemn you as a threat."

I ripped my head from his grip and collapsed to the floor. Breathing heavily while looking up to Him, my eyes bled fear. I tried to scream for Mr. Rassenberg but remained choked and voiceless.

"Please, my son, this is an enlightening. I have always wanted the pleasure of opening a mortal's eyes at such a young age. It will take you to places unimaginable. You will be free of His pressures; you will live a free life. I admire the hate you have created inside yourself. Please, take my hand." I grabbed his inviting hand and pulled myself up, wiping small tears slowly appearing under my eyes. "Your parents consumed you with religion, but did not care to use humane exercises while raising you. They made you feel worthless, never good enough, am I right?" The man squinted his piercing eyes, and although he needn't a reply; he waited for one.

With a forced sigh I replied with, "yes" and continued to remain quiet. The power surging through me was relentless. The images still piercing the nerves in my brain. The man placed a hand on my shoulder and squeezed gently.

"I come from a place where sin is breathed in through light. Condemned not, we consider ourselves self-ruling. I have created a world of truth for my followers. Consider this a type of recruitment. I have looked deep inside your soul, young man. The pain you feel can also be mine. I do not abandon, I give what is deserved, and those that serve me are guaranteed a spot in my kingdom. I am not tedious, you do not have to worship, just believe the truth that your God is false. He beckons people to serve His will, yet shows no interest in yours. His kingdom is failing, and I will soon reign over *all* of His domain. Take a look at my world." The man squeezed harder on my shoulder, more images forcefully engaging my thoughts.

It was dark, and a group of people stood around a burning crucifix as a bloodied man was brutally pinned to it. The group of people shouted, cursed, and laughed, their eyes full of black. As I stood there in the middle of the crowd, the ground cracked open, billowing smoke and giving way. Below the ruptured ground, a pool of naked bodies fornicated while their skin slowly melted together.

The air filled with the moans of their sexual souls in the depths.

A desirable woman began to clamber toward me from the earth beneath. She was naked and covered in a dark mud, her breasts swinging as she crawled closer yet. Her hand nestled on my crotch, caressing it as her expression turned a raw sensual. The man's voice flooded my ears from a far distance, "I can give you anything your sinful heart desires. I can help you proclaim your darkest secrets, and embrace your inner fantasies. Never go back to Him. Hell will bring you overwhelming pleasure."

I shifted back to the tailor shop, my skin painted with sweat, and tears draining from my eyes. The man was towering over me as I lay crumpled on the floor at His feet. He extended His hand with a smirk. I closed my eyes once more and gripped the hand that now felt cold and skeletal. The world around me came back into focus as I stood upright. The cold sweat evaporating immediately from my skin.

"It feels like the world has changed you, I know. You must understand the meaning behind my actions. If I reveal to you, you must endure everything." His smirk faded, revealing a sternness that actually showed concern.

"No more visions, please." I doubled over, holding my hand up in protest. It was pure mercy that was shown next by the now growling man.

"You are already changed, my son. You will see me again. Maybe in your dreams, maybe in person. But forever changed you are."

That day, he walked out without ever buying a suit. I know deep down he had come there for me all along. It was as if I was His one and only mission for that day.

Now, the only time I ever hear the man's voice is when I'm taking a life, and many lives I have taken indeed. I think I do it out of gratefulness to my savior for showing me the true way.

The only way.

I hope to see him again...someday.

# On Edge

Officer Brandt held his breath and clenched his eyes shut. The anxiety was almost too much to bear. But, it was good anxiety. Relieving anxiety. A monster was about to go to his rightful place – the lowest possible layer of Hell.

He made sure it was all lined up perfectly. He made sure to tell the precinct that he could carry out the arrest on his own and backup was unnecessary. This piece of shit was not going to get the luxury of being arrested.

Robert Brandt was going to make sure of that.

Robert had been following the case carefully since the allegations were made by the perp's thirteen year old daughter. She had confided in her biology teacher that her father was wrongfully acting out sexually towards her. Although now it was only fondling taking place behind closed doors, sooner or later his actions would become bolder.

Robert sat impatiently in his undercover Buick squad car, gazing at the old farmhouse Mr. Wylowski called home. The white paint around the house chipped to an *almost* shiny dull grey, the boards broken and replaced with mismatched panels. It looked like a backwoods cannibal's wet dream. No one was home, the house was empty. Soon he would be home from work, unknowingly entering a world of pain.

He reached for the glovebox and yanked out the warrant sheet. In big, bold letters that stood out loudly was JIM WYLOWSKI: ORDER OF ARREST. As much as Robert loved the look of it in a sentence, that punishment would be too easy to endure.

Suddenly out of nowhere, a baseball flew from overtop the car, landing in front with a bouncing thud. He saw a little boy running towards it with a baseball glove three sizes too big. He remembered that red and white baseball shirt – he used to wear it any given chance he could. A tall man followed behind the boy, bearing a grin of both amusement and possible boredom. It was a mask; this man did not enjoy whatsoever spending time with his son.

The man stopped behind the boy and placed a

hand on his shoulder. Robert remembered this conversation, the conversation that started all conversations. The boy looked up at his father, waiting for him to speak. The sparkle of innocence shined bright around the child, the innocence that in the next couple of hours would be lost forever.

"This playing catch stuff is getting old, buddy. Wanna do something a little more fun?" Now the grin was a full blown smile, with a radiation magnitude of a barrel of bio-genetically engineered formula. "I got something I would like to show you." Within the car, within another world, Robert watched the boy's curiosity spark with a glow.

"Of course, Dad!" Why wouldn't the boy agree? It's his father – flesh and blood. Doesn't a child place full trust in a parent? The dreadful walk into the fire of no return.

Robert saw the events that followed, the disgusting acts of pleasing 'Dad'. He cringed his face tightly and reached once more into the glovebox, this time pulling out a pint of cheap whiskey. He swigged it back, trying to get the image of his father's cock out of his head. Whiskey always replaced the mourning with anger. A good thing for a day like this.

After the second swig, Robert now saw a teenaged boy walk across the front of the car, wearing a football jersey with 30 in big, red numbers. The boy looked solemn, disappointed, and Robert knew how this was going to play out also. He shook his head to try and clear the memory, but the boy was still visible out front. His father jokingly ran up from behind, lightly charging forward into his son. The kid mustered a fake giggle and immediately switched his expression back to glum.

"What's got you so down, buddy?" He masqueraded his monster and replaced it with a dad with no worries in the world. It was always a stage show performance. "Anything I can do?" The statement sounded more sinister than it should have.

"No, Dad, I'm fine." The boy could barely speak the word *Dad*; it was a poisoning word that caused flash floods of emotions.

The dad smiled brightly again and lowered himself down to his son's level.

"You know I can make you feel better." He transformed now, this was the Devil that emerged from the closet. This was the creature underneath the bed.

"I said I'm fine!" The boy lurched forward, shoving him backward and onto his ass. He leaped into a full sprint before tripping over his own feet, only yards away from his father.

"All I do for you and this is how you treat me, you little son of a bitch!" His father blurted while gaining his feet. "Do I have to properly show you how to act again!?"

Robert placed his face in his hands and wept; he could not watch anymore. He already knew the story and there was not a happy ending.

"Unit 4-3, we need clearance on the matter. 4-3, do you need backup?"

Robert snapped back to reality, with fresh tears streaming to stickiness around his rosy red cheeks. He grabbed the radio in reflex.

"Dispatch, this is unit 4-3, waiting on the assailant to arrive home. No backup needed. I'll confirm as soon as the arrest is made. Over." Only, no arrest was being made and dispatch would most likely never hear from Robert again. The thought somewhat scared him. He was not afraid of death per se, but the thought of non-existence – the thought of being nothing – which does basically translate to fear of death.

He saw himself on the day his father died. It was a rainy mess of thunderstorms that ended one of the biggest storms in Robert's life. He remembered hearing his father's voice that early morning call out to him in desperation. At first, Robert awoke in panic, until the thought hit him like a wave of refreshment. What if the monster was dying? What if everything loathsome ends today, with his father? He sat in bed with a smile on his face, listening intently for more desperate requests for his aid.

Finally deciding to get out of bed and investigate, Robert found his father in the kitchen, clenching his chest. Robert did not have time to react before his father fell to the ground with sounds of gurgled soup erupting from his throat, followed by gasps for air. Calmly, Robert walked back up to his bedroom with one thought in his mind – *I'll deal with it later. No chance of survival then.*

Afternoon came and Robert was not proved a

liar. His father had died of a massive heart attack. With much remorse, the paramedics said he suffocated on his saliva. Robert felt none of the remorse projected from the paramedics. He was glad he was dead, along with all of his heinous acts. *Irony is that you choked, just as you forcibly choked your son with that nasty piece of flesh dangled between your now rotting legs.*

At the age of nineteen, he was given the house despite much protest. He didn't want to live there a second longer. The emotional power his father had over him now vanquished, it was time to leave the last of it behind. He moved out two months after his death with much hope for the future. But the scars never faded.

Deep down, Robert knew this day was coming, from the moment he joined the police academy. Now, 26 years later, this perfect opportunity lay before him. The time of the clock read 3:42 PM, he had been waiting for nearly an hour. He should be home any time now. Robert swigged another mouthful of whisky and winced. The day's work had just begun.

As if an answer came from his prayers, an old rusted pickup truck pulled behind his squad car. A sudden excitement knocked on Robert's chest like a kid picked first in kickball. The man sprang from the truck almost instantly, and Robert followed.

"What's this all about?" He was a grungy, bearded man with a 'These Colors Don't Bleed' ball cap that presented an American flag. Only his had more brown than red.

"Mr. Wylowski, I've been waiting a good minute on you!" In no way, shape, or form, did the tone sound threatening, quite the opposite. "I'm afraid I have a bit of bad news for you." Robert drew his pistol and kept it held at waistline. The bearded man chuckled and approached closer.

"Is this a joke? Did Kevin put you up to this?"

"Oh I'm afraid I don't know a Kevin. This is far from a joke, Mr. Wylowski. I'm pretty sure your daughter wouldn't laugh either." The statement stung the man into realization of the matter. His face flipped upside down. The left strap of his overalls slid down as his shoulders slouched in defeat.

"I have an arrest warrant for you, Mr. Wylowski, but that isn't the bad news."

Wylowski smirked at the comment while taking another step forward.

"Oh yeah? Well then, what's the bad news?"

"The bad news is that your arrest warrant is futile, because I'm going to fucking kill you."

The repugnant man chuckled once more, still not accepting the situation as fact. He needed a bit more convincing. Robert raised his Beretta and pointed it to the man's head. Wylowski flinched slightly, taking a step back.

"What the fuck is going on here? What are you really doing here?" His frown proved he was taking the situation more seriously. The smell of chewing tobacco and beer radiated from his breath, even from a distance.

Robert raised a finger in signal to wait one second.

"Here, Mr. Wylowski, I'll show you." He went to the car and pulled out the warrant, raising it in the air as if in triumph. "See here, you dickless sack of shit? I have a warrant for your arrest for fondling your goddam daughter. But I figured killing you would be more proper. Sickos like you don't deserve the luxury of being arrested."

Wylowski lurched forward with an out-of-shape effort. Robert responded with a gunshot to his right knee cap. The man screamed in pain, holding his wound as his hat fell to the ground.

"You fuck! You shot me!"

"There's plenty more pain where that came from, sicko." Robert looked to the tool shed behind the house that resembled more of a dilapidated shack, the roof caved inward at the middle. "I think I just found your place of demise, my friend."

With the grip of his pistol, Robert sprang forward and swung the weapon downward on top of the man's balding head. He was unconscious within seconds.

The fun was about to begin.

The water splashed Wylowski's face with a powerful blast, awakening him instantly in a frantic panic. He did not immediately notice his surroundings, as he blinked his focusing eyes around the environment in confusion. It wasn't long before he realized he was in his own tool shed. Robert was standing proudly in front of him with a wide smile, holding an impact drill. He pulled the drill trigger and laughed maniacally. Wylowski could not focus on anything except the rotating bit, shining brightly under the single hanging lamp above them.

"Glad you could make it, I was beginning to think you weren't ever going to wake up."

Robert could see his dad inside Wylowski. The same tormenting eyes that worked so well in convincing the innocent. The poignant aroma of sick sexual perversion emanated from his skin just as he remembered his father's did. He was a flashback from Hell, only this time Robert changed the outcome.

For a split second, behind Wylowski, he saw himself at the age of 15. He was beaten and bloodied, holding his knees in the fetal position, wearing only his underwear plagued with dirt stains. His father came home drunk that night, and his son was the entree for dinner. His father's words echoed around the room like an approaching jet. *You use teeth again, you will get them knocked out!*

"I bet you hate it when she uses teeth, don't

you? Your own fucking daughter!"

Wylowski winced visibly at the accusation. He finally looked down to see himself tied to an old wooden chair. His wrists bled from the friction of the tightened rope.

"I don't know who you are or what you think I did but…"

"She went to a teacher, told them everything. Your wife sang too, but to the precinct. Seems you have a couple of priors concerning sexual misconduct. It didn't take much to get the warrant confirmed. Once I knew it was all in place, I began planning your death. And now, here we are!" Robert held out his arms, still gripping the drill tightly. The enjoyment on his face was blatantly obvious, like a maniac beyond his last breaking point. It scared Wylowski to the core, just as Robert intended.

"Listen, I can give you money to stop this. Anything you want, I can get." He closed his eyes tightly, panting heavily. He was on the verge of a panic attack. "You don't have to do this. They have been lying for years! They have always slated against me!"

Robert sprinted forward and planted his left foot into the dead center of Wylowski's chest, catapulting him backwards in his chair. His head smacked the concrete floor with a nasty thud.

"No more lies!" Robert screamed, now realizing the tears streaming down his face. It was hard not to be deceived by such persuading creatures. The voice is always the most toxic, spilling lies and sin within every syllable uttered. Wylowski moaned in anguish, moving his bound feet up and down slowly at the tips.

Robert hovered over the dazed man as he looked up, confused. "Keep spreading those lies and I'll put one in your head right now."

Robert remembered to contact dispatch so no unwelcome visitors would arrive. He would tell them that Wylowski still had not returned home and he would only be willing to stay another hour on this stakeout. By then, the both of them would be dead. He made sure the precinct told the man's family to leave for the night, and they did just that.

The air was fresh as Robert stepped outside. The birds chirped proudly into the blaring sun that would soon be going down. It was a beautiful day for such a horrifying outcome. But not all of it was horrifying, redemption had to be somewhere in the event of killing a monster.

He went to his squad car and grabbed the radio for the last time.

"Dispatch, come in, this is 4-3. Over." He waited blankly for a response that took roughly four seconds.

"Copy 4-3. Over." It was Melanie on the dispatch today. He could picture her on the other side of the line, gripping her coffee cup with her old, withered fingers while holding one side of her head set. It comically never fit well on her outdated permed hair.

"Still waiting for the perp at the Wylowski's residence. Another hour or so, I'm calling it." He made his voice sound bored and impatient. Convincing was the key, after all.

"Copy that, 4-3"

That was all he needed to hear. He promptly returned to the tool shed. He saw himself once more, next to its entrance, smiling happily while sitting cross legged. It was days after his father's death and he could remember the joy he felt at his demise – a feeling of absolute freedom. His life had just begun, and the possibilities were endless. The boy did not see the vast sea of memories that would plague and destroy him on a regular basis. Robert smiled at the vision of his young self as he slowly faded to nothing.

"I'll free us once more, my friend."

Wylowski was wide awake, moaning consistently with an occasional attempted cry for help.

"Is that you making all that noise?" He was still lying on his back with the chair held to him tightly. It was one of the most appeasing scenes Robert had ever seen.

"Let me go, you fuckin' psycho!" His voice was coarse with strain.

"But we haven't started our fun yet. Just imagine yourself now, as your daughter. Bound and unable to move while some monster has their way with you. Think of your daughter!"

It enraged him to the maximum; he needed to inflict pain. Robert snatched the drill and placed

Wylowski back up in position. He watched in terror as Robert slowly applied the drill to his right thigh. Blood shot up in strings as the man's screams overtook the scenery. Next, the drill eyed the man's crotch, moving closer to it in slow, impending doom.

As the drill-bit reached the clothing at his scrotum region, the cloth twisted up within the drill. Robert plunged the drill forward, puncturing perfectly in-between his two testicles. Thick, dark red fluid, along with Wylowski's ripped open sack, gushed out of his pants and down his shaking legs. Wylowski's eyes faded dim as he went in and out of consciousness. His screams diminished into low, coughing gags.

"Better stay awake for this one. Finally making that tool of disgust as useless as you are."

Robert pulled a pair of pliers from his back pocket and went for Wylowski's dick, which hung out partially from the torn and bloodied cloth. He should have done this savagery to his father years ago, instead of having him respectfully taken by a natural cause of death. The feeling within him was retribution at the highest of levels. It was a victim gaining closure from the destroyed life of a creature of the night. A victim has to become the villain in the end. There is no other way to gain justice.

Robert grabbed the head of Wylowski's dick with the pliers and steadily pulled. The flap of skin stretched outward, creating redness in the pale flesh. The veins along the shaft disappeared into the retracting foreskin. Wylowski's panting became primitive and desperate. The small penis stretched to around six inches before ripping grotesquely at the middle. The skin made a wet, tearing sound as blood erupted violently, splattering to the concrete.

Further, Robert stretched with a smile, until the last attachment of membrane tore off. He waved the dangling cock in front of Wylowski's barely alive face trying to focus. Blood continuously flowed like a river of salvation.

"I should have saved that for last. You're about dead from bleeding out."

As Wylowski's brain somehow plunged its way back into reality, he realized the extent of the madness upon him and started screaming wildly. Robert now wielded a screwdriver he held out like a titan slasher in an 80's flick.

"Going to need you to bend over for this one." Robert pushed Wylowski from the side, tipping him over. He lifted him onto his face with his ass up in the air, between the back and bottom of the chair. "You know that expression *stick it up your ass*? Well-hell, I'll just show you." He stabbed the screwdriver down into the man's tightened rectum. The last scream escaped Wylowski's salivating mouth.

The screwdriver went deep enough to stop at the handle, and Robert jimmied it back and forth – creating squishy audibles that sounded a lot like grapes smashing. Robert was surprised at the ease with which the screwdriver was penetrating his asshole through a layer of pants and underwear. It was all meant to be – it was loudly apparent.

With a final tearing noise and a fountain of discharged blood, the stretched diameter of the hole could nicely fit a golf ball. The gurgling in Wylowski's throat indicated he did not have much longer to go. Robert would let him bleed out from his sexual organs in a kind of sick and twisted irony.

Robert saw himself over the dying Wylowski,

holding his issued Beretta, at just the tender age of five or six. The expression on the little boy's face was hope, a small shape of it. He knew the message the boy was conveying. The last piece of the puzzle for the prize of freedom. Robert took the pistol from the boy's held out hand and looked deep into his imploring gaze. Tears swelled up within both sets of eyes and they both reclaimed peace among themselves.

Does redemption claim over damnation, when it is evil that is destroyed?

No one will ever know the truth; they can only strive forward for answers to one's peace of mind. Robert placed the pistol under his chin and pulled the trigger.

I guess sometimes, you have to be damned to be reclaimed.

# Fender Bender

The mornings, it seems, are always the worst.

The flood gates of memories crumble down at first wake, filling your head with unwilling torment. For Jason Desmoines, it all goes back to that one phone call. Being a single parent can claim hectic to any human being, but Jason was not always a single parent. No. The phone call made him one and created a storm that permanently hung above his head. The maniac on the other line took one of the most precious things in his life.

Jason shifted in bed while mustering up the courage to start another day. The sun was not shining (thankfully), and the pitter patter of raindrops could be softly heard from his bedroom window. Maddox was awake in the kitchen; he could hear her making her own breakfast for the morning. He felt guilty for his negligence, but sometimes there's that excuse which somehow can prove valid. He was quite surprised Maddox had not checked on him yet – it was fifteen minutes after the usual wake up time.

He rose from his bed slowly, feeling the headache from last night's booze session. He shuddered as his feet hit the cold, wooden floor.

*Black rose, left shoulder.*

Those four words incinerated inside Jason's mind – burning scars that could not be removed. He knew someday he would find the black rose. The last words of his oldest daughter had to serve great purpose. It was the final puzzle piece he obsessed about.

"Daddy, you up?" This was followed by three knocks on the bedroom door. His blurry mind began to shift back into focus.

"Yes beautiful, I'm up." Jason said as a grin formed. He felt like saying more, but nothing came to him. Losing a child and wife in one year can make you unsociable, even to your seven year old daughter. He had called off his dealings with God, what was the use for Him? It wasn't Him keeping Jason alive, it was Maddox.

He walked to the door in strain, feeling as if his eighty year birthday party was tomorrow. An excited Maddox greeted him proudly with a strong hug around his waist.

"Tonight's the night!" she screamed with cheer and she bounced on her tiptoes. It was the night of her ballet recital and honestly, he had forgotten. He made sure and did not show it on his face. Instead, he smiled wider.

"I know, honey, you're going to be amazing, sweetheart." A burst of unrelenting love shined off of his heart. She was the only one who could do that these days.

Maddox let go of his waist and headed back for the kitchen in a skip. "Better hurry, Dad, you got up late. We have about fifteen minutes until we gotta go. Can you give me a ride to school? I hate riding the bus on rainy days like this."

Jason was taken aback at her maturity; it reminded him of Sage. Maddox continued getting her things together while glowing with joy. Seeing her like this was damn near impossible to not grant any wish she requested. Except maybe, to bring her big sister back. He headed for the kitchen also, hearing the coffee machine bubbling with the day's caffeine source.

"Of course I will give my little ballerina a ride. You making me coffee now, huh?" He made sure to not sound too sarcastic. After the death of her sister and mother, her sensitivity levels were off the charts, escalating further each day.

"I've seen you do it enough times to do it myself. No big deal." She looked like a grown business woman eating her cereal. All she needed to further push the look was the day's paper sitting in front of her face.

Jason only shook his head, still smiling. "Okay, babe. Going to get dressed real quick." He walked to his bedroom once more, closing the door behind him.

Today was a typical day, plagued with bad thoughts. It was blood-curdling to replay the scenario repeatedly in his head over and over again, but on days like these, he had no choice. It all started with Sage asking to go to a friend's house for a sleepover. Most potently, he remembered the smile on his oldest daughter's face before she left – the last time he had seen her alive. She was sixteen, and for Jason and his wife Karen, the teenage years for Sage were not all that drama-filled or stressful. In fact, the night before Sage was murdered, Jason and his wife talked about their luck with such a respectable and trustworthy daughter they had raised.

It felt good (ironically) to see other parents struggle with their teens, only for them to get through it gracefully, with the help from Sage of course. But that smile. The smile that reminded him so much of his wife; that told a thousand stories of happiness, strength, and the utmost compassion. Now it just haunted him. At the time before Sage's death, Jason's life had all the meaning he wanted it to have. Maddox had just turned six, and he had the full love of his family. That was before it all blew away on the winds of misery.

The phone rang at 1AM that night and it was Jason who answered it. He remembered feeling dread as soon as the first ring loudly broadcasted from his cell phone on the nightstand next to him. The commotion in the background still echoed through his eardrums as a hideous reminder of how helpless a father truly can be in the most sinister of situations.

The scream came next, followed by the four words that he repeated over and over in his head a thousand times a day.

*Black rose, left shoulder.*

His breath was sucked away instantly in fright as three sudden knocks banged outside his bedroom door. He discovered himself staring in the mirror, tears streaming down his red, irritated eyes.

"Dad, hurry up! I'm ready!"

He quickly wiped his tears as if hiding guilty evidence. "Be right there, honey." His voice was shaky, something he could not hide. He quickly threw on his clothes and met his anxious daughter, still waiting outside his bedroom door. Ten minutes later, they were headed out the door – ten minutes too late, according to Maddox.

The rain had picked up since Jason had awakened. Maddox held her hands to the air, catching the raindrops on her tiny palms. The vibe of the gloomy day thankfully tucked the horrors of Jason's mind under his belt a bit. The happiness of his daughter was a plus for his depleting sanity.

Raindrops accumulated on the windshield

during the drive as Jason's thoughts began to wander towards the darkness of reality.

*Black rose, left shoulder.*

"Wipers, Dad. Too much rain on the window." The constant supervision brought a welcoming smile to his face as he shined it back at his daughter in the rearview mirror. She immediately went back to tapping her feet and humming.

He decided to turn the radio on to keep him focused on the road. He thought of work and how in an hour and a half he would have to be at the lumberyard, a job he obtained five months prior. It paid the bills, but barely sufficient. His days as a realtor were long gone.

Maddox's smile reminded him to contact Detective Franks after dropping her off – as a failed attempt occurred the night before. Finding the person who brutally murdered your daughter may seem like an easy enough task for any parent, but nothing could be further from the truth. There were no leads on anything after a year and discouragement pounded rapidly on Jason's soul.

The assailant cleaned his tracks masterfully

before leaving the scene. Sage and her friend Allison died from a malicious beating with a lead pipe; detectives hurriedly forwarded that they had not been sexually assaulted (as if that makes it better for a parent). After the bastard beat them, he strung them up by two black, leather belts.

*Black rose.....*

"Turn the song up Dad, please." Maddox said calmly and continued her low hum.

*Left shoulder.....*

Jason turned the volume up on the radio and tried to concentrate on the music. The school came up on the right, almost impossible to see as it emerged like a shadow in the mist. The thick fog from the precipitation partially obscured children and parents walking up to the building. Jason pulled under the clearing outside the front doors. The private school required uniforms for the children while the place itself resembled an old psychiatric hospital. The steel awning out front was the most expensive thing on the building.

"Did you bring your umbrella, hun?" Jason said, turning to the back seat. Maddox answered with a quick yes, a wave of the hand, and a see you later. She walked with a frantic pace, her long skirt shifting in the brisk breeze with her ashy brown hair until she was inside the building.

Jason's mind went to a certain medicine hidden in the glovebox. He paused for a moment, looking around suspiciously for possible eyes on his actions. He quickly reached for the compartment and grabbed the small pint of memory suppressant stashed under the car's registration papers. He immediately took a big swig, the harshness both caressing and tart.

The first gulp always brought back the memories he tried so desperately to overcome – as if it was giving him one last blast of truth. The second gulp left thoughts mildly vibrant, becoming dampered. The third gulp put everything below the waistline – keeping his head fogged to perfection. Jason took a fourth gulp to play it safe. He threw the liquor back in its sacred place and put the car in drive.

The rain had died down to an occasional sprinkle. The clouds came and went like the fleeting thoughts of one's mind. As Jason arrived back home, a growing ray of sunshine forced its way through the fading clouds. The dull aftertaste of the memory suppression was lingering on Jason's taste buds.

Jason's first obligation was to call Detective Franks before heading out for work. The last time they had talked was two weeks beforehand. Jason demanded an update on the investigation into the tattoo database in the police records. The words *black rose, left shoulder* had to have a deeper meaning, and the one that made most sense was the description of the fucker's tattoo. The tattoo had not been in the system prior to the murders, but the possibility of getting picked up eventually could be the key.

*Black rose, left shoulder...*

He had to be out there somewhere. During the incident, the Macomb Police Department investigated all over the U.S, calling into out-of-state departments for tattoo records. It was an everyday fight, and for a little while Jason had a partner to help – his wife. Karen was strong with hope at first. The slow decline of her spirit was a devastating sight to behold, and the will for survival deemed impossible for her. As the investigation dug deeper with no results for Sage's murder, Karen saw closure only in death.

The devastation of losing Sage reigned supreme on all of their hearts. Maddox suffered the loss as a new meaning to life, and after her mom was dead, a permanent damage was held within. How do you explain such tragedies to a six year old? You tell them the brutal truth. No sense in sugar-coating, when the world around us is far from comforting. She became bitter of the fact, a tormenting trait that resided in the both of them. She was just better at hiding it.

Jason sat his phone on the kitchen table and glared at it blankly, contemplating the point of even calling the detective. Deep down, in the pit of his stomach, he felt the news already. Nothing had changed, and nothing would – until Jason did something about it himself. The web of deceit the killer left behind seemed indecipherable, and everyone out to capture him had been stumped with no clues.

Weeks after the murders, Detective Franks would not let the case rest for one moment, and his perseverance was promising at first. Franks had a daughter around the same age as Sage and he had taken it as a deadly sin that needed purifying. But everyone loses hope eventually and after months went by with nothing to move on, his motivation decreased immensely. The last weeks, he had not even bothered returning Jason's unrelenting phone calls.

Jason picked up the phone, holding it in his hand like a rare gem, discovered for the first time ever by a human's eyes.

Detective John Franks sat at his polished oak desk, tapping his ink pen gently against the side of his temple. The past years' cases had piled up to an unwanted heap. As he focused on the stacked case files on his desk, he swore he could hear the faint sound of all the victims held within the unsolved papers. Fathers, Mothers, Sons, Daughters, the list went on in a disgraceful world of murder. If God was intended to create protection among His creations, He should probably find a different profession.

The world was as dark as it could possibly get (he hoped), and truthfully, he would rather be doing anything besides gazing at the files of cases that will most probably never see justice. Dead trees with information concerning destroyed life, that is what lay in front of him. Was it cliché to want to be the unlikely hero who finally brings forth punishment to the people who no longer could get the justice they deserved? A fast spreading obsession that often held a firm grip developed, but sometimes you have to let go.

The loud buzz of his cell phone broke his morbid concentration. He reached quickly for his belt out of reflex – knowing partially with naive precognition who it was going to be. He was correct, and the words JASON DESMOINES shined brightly into his tired eyes. He placed the phone down on his desk and let it vibrate annoyingly until it abruptly stopped. The fuel of the fire needed to cool off. Sure it seemed like a cop out (no pun intended), and maybe even for a detective, but there was a necessity of evil in the world, and if his torture balanced that, then so be it.

Like a creature from the darkness, plagued with revenge, a blast of memory smashed its way into the core of Jason's brain. Panicky, he ran for his secret stash under the kitchen sink. One more mind flush to do the trick. He had grown an immunity to alcohol and he'd rather finally put the bullet in his head instead of choosing hard drugs. The swig went down quick and smooth, as it always now did.

Jason took a deep breath and dropped to one knee while placing his hand on the cold kitchen floor for balance. He saw a flash of Sage, standing upright. Her skin had turned a purplish blue, with small and large boils from decomposition. A belt wrapped tightly around her neck. Her mouth leaked a shiny black ooze that resembled thick car oil. Her eyes bared a pain no living being could possibly imagine.

Jason squinted his eyes and pushed on them with his free hand.

"Please, please stop..." Had his ears not begun to ring blaringly, he would have heard himself pathetically whimper. Tears slowly leaked from his closed lids, it was inevitable. He released the grip against his eyeballs, and opened them cautiously. Sage was no longer there, but the puddle of ooze was, spreading like an out of control oil spill. The pace of its spread was unnatural and headed right for Jason.

He threw himself back urgently, slamming his head against the cabinet door behind him. Hands emerged from the goo when it came within range. Dripping with black, the only color was the pink on her fingernails.

Jason began to scream.

A man sat parked in his 1974, rusted, black pickup truck, quietly observing. It was a Ford and he wouldn't have had it any other way. His Dad used to say, "You never get BORED with a FORD." He supposed not, he hadn't been bored since he found his new found strength in life. A strength that set him free from judgement, and the will to do whatever needed to be done to better accommodate himself.

The truck was parked outside a two story suburban home, nicely sided with a freshly mown lawn. He was across the street, tucked back, so no suspicions could occur. But it wasn't the house that concerned him, it was the teenage girl in front of it, dragging a garbage bag with a protruding backpack hunched on top of her. Her thighs jiggled to the beat of her stomps in a rhythmic tune which only he could hear – he liked that. He would make sure her thighs jiggle when he was on top of her, beating her.

Would he beat this one? He hadn't thought about it, but the time to start was now. Planning may be a pain in the ass, but ultimately necessary. He had been watching the house closely for almost two weeks, and the pattern of the family's routine was nicely laid out in front of him within the examining time. Her parents (yuppies) liked to leave on a Friday or Saturday night – he didn't know why (probably to hang out with other yuppies), but he didn't fucking care. It would leave him the perfect window to do what needed to be done.

The man unconsciously began to rub his hardening crotch. He gripped the steering wheel with confused emotion and melted into his seat, moaning softly. If her parents followed suit and left tonight, it would be the perfect time for the crime. Perfect time for a crime – that rhymed. The man laughed at himself, breaking his sexual trance. He looked around with a fogged head. The teenage girl was already halfway down the street with a pip to her step as she walked to school. He sighed deeply and threw the truck into drive. He would be back at dusk.

Detective Franks stood outside the interrogation room with a disgusted look on his face, blaring an annoyed glare at the culprit inside. He would much rather put a bullet in the sick asshole's head instead of the same ol' bullshit "who dunnit" act.

Mario Ramirez was being charged with four counts of aggravated sexual assault with a deadly weapon. The man apparently thought consent was for the weak, and so he would take any woman he wanted by threatening their lives with a butcher knife. He had quite the reputation, which emitted a boastful energy around him. He sat at the far end of the table, rolling his head back and forth.

Detective Aubree Snow approached behind Frank. She was a pleasant looking woman with olive skin and more tattoos than one could count in a single sitting. Snow had just received her detective shield two weeks prior, and the routine abound was still fresh in the making. She handed Franks a Styrofoam cup of coffee, still billowing steam from the top.

"Thought you could use this before you go in." She shot him a smirk and looked at the sexual deviant waiting in the room. "What a sick fuck. I hope to fuck we nail him to the wall this time. Fucking monster..." Her lipped curled, revealing pearly white teeth. Franks took a quick swig of the coffee and slammed it on the desk beside him. Java splashed out in scattered tiny dots.

"Well, I guess I oughta try nailing him to the wall." Franks smiled and walked into the room, sighing heavily upon closing the door behind him.

Mario halted rolling his head and smiled menacingly. Two large diamond tattoos resided under both his eyes. He was in a 'wife beater' with a montage of naked women in different sexual positions along his arms like sleeves. If there was one thing being a detective had ever taught Franks, it was to ALWAYS let the suspect talk first. Their first sentence in the interrogation always held more keys than imaginable. The suspects who demanded lawyers instantly always proved in some way or another, they had something to hide. It is human nature to confront anxiety with a worthy protection source.

Mario did not say a word, only kept eye contact with a slow burning smirk. John decided he would not engage in the staring contest and went right in with the first words.

"So, raping girls is your M.O. huh?" John said, sitting down and clearing his throat sarcastically. Mario chuckled but remained quiet.

"Go ahead, don't speak. We have three people willing to testify on your scum ass." John leaned forward to invoke a sense of intimidation. He didn't have three people to testify, he needed this confession once and for all. "By the time I'm done with you, that disgusting flap you call a dick will never be able to destroy another life again."

Mario also leaned forward, matching John's wit. "If you had proof, I would not be sitting here in this room right now. And for the record, destroyed lives? Please. They love this cock."

John tried with everything to push the anger deep inside him. It was ticking in the darkest parts of his being, withering to a point of no return. The emotions erupted from his skin volcanically. He lunged forward over the table, grabbing Mario by the throat in a primal instinct. Further down, some place unknown inside John, lurked the thought of the time he severely beat his stepfather. He could see the look on his stepfather's face, the same as Mario's, frozen in utter surprised panic where the possibility of escape is at the forefront of one's mind.

Detective Snow rushed in, and before John knew it, she was pulling him off strenuously. Franks regained composure after a smack to his cranium on the hard linoleum floor, Detective Snow panting heavily next to him. Mario huffed and puffed while rubbing his throat, tears streaming from his strained eyes. The memory of John's stepfather escaped as quickly as it came; he would hold it deep inside him until his own demise.

Detective Franks caught his breath and left the room. He had fucked up the confession beyond belief.

Jason sat on a stump outside the headquarters of Limberg's Lumber, sipping black coffee and embracing the nasty consequences of coming down off of alcohol. Work was busy, and the hard work was plenty, but Jason could not get his head right. Bad days came often, but left a deeper scar each time.

He thought of Maddox and hoped she was enjoying her day at school, excited for her ballet recital. He imagined her at lunch, sitting with her friends, laughing about the crazy stories recent cartoons had evoked. He saw her munching on her favorite foods: chicken nuggets, green beans, and chocolate pudding. Sure, no school could create such a perfect meal for a particular kid's taste, but that's what makes imaginations so appealing.

It could bring a smile when nothing else in the world is worth smiling for. Jason did smile, wide and full, and a little giggle even escaped his lips. He chuckled in the mid-day breeze, watching the sky's dark clouds roll backward, bringing in occasional sunlight. He had about ten minutes left of his break and only dread lay ahead; he needed a piece of serenity.

As he put his head down, embracing his futile happiness, a glimpse of darkness followed. Sage appeared in his head, the belt around her throat was tight. She could not breathe, she clawed while gagging. Her eyes bulged to the pulse of her beating heart. It was the kind of suffering nightmares were made of. Before the vision ceased, Jason was off the stump, curled in the grass. The escaping sunlight reached him swiftly, sucking him out of his Hell. He hastily got to his feet and headed to his car. A mind flush was mandatory for normal functioning.

*Sick fuck. You worthless piece of nothing. You're sick. Sick fuck.* The man grabbed his head and strained every muscle in his body. It felt tense inside him, the urges slowly taking their course to the eventual outcome. It happened like this every time. The need to unleash every ounce of hate and despair left inside. It was a brutal fetish of releasement. He took a small kitchen knife and slowly moved it to his chest, still tense to the bone. He pressed the blade above his right nipple and applied strength. Slowly, blood escaped the forming cut.

The pain felt nourishing, but meek. He needed the real thing. Blood was nothing until it told a horrifying story. Blood left his skin and entered his penis; it throbbed to a maddening hardness. He would make sure and not ejaculate this time. No, that was not the acceptable thing to do in the moment of shine. Only sick fucks would do something so horrendous in the most glorious of times. Taking a life was spiritual. The sacrifice of purity was a miracle of great magnitude and not to be taken lightly. It was time to head home and begin planning.

Detective Franks sat in the police precinct break room, intently watching the clock above him in fresh sweat. It had been a helluva day, and Franks needed to go home and put a fork in it. Police officers passing through glanced his way and whispered under their breath. He had been the talk of the department for the fifth time now, and he was sure there would be a sixth. When life crumbles, the best thing to do is crumble with it. It was out of his hands just as much as anyone else. The clock read 3:45, fifteen minutes to a much needed departure. He breathed in stale air and held his breath to calm his vibrating nerves. It was a full blown approaching panic attack, something he had learned to deal with on the regular.

"You okay, boss?"

Franks turned around unenthusiastically to the soft, feminine voice of Snow. She looked just as worn as him, her white frosted hair stuck up in strands from the previous commotion. Her eyes looked like recent tears had fallen.

"Getting there. You alright? Didn't mean to

upset you so." He was being honest, the roughness of her exterior made him feel guilty. She was new to the shithole, no need to make it worse for her as she herself was realizing the mistakes of her career choices. Franks tried to manage a smirk but his face refused to respond.

"Yeah, I'll deal with it. Just another day at the office, right?" Snow did manage a smirk, but far from believable. It told a face of denial, a denial of torment we all encounter one way or another.

Franks did not reply back, he had nothing to say. He instead lowered his head, as statement enough for lack of words. She followed suit and looked down to her feet. Before he knew it, Franks was alone in the room again. He got up sluggishly and flicked on the TV hanging in the corner of the room. The channel showed news of murder, society's favorite topic of all. Franks giggled to himself and sat back down, keeping his eyes on the screen.

Ten more minutes and it's home free, one of the very few things to look forward to recently. He felt disgust in himself, how he let his anger and fear control him the way it did earlier. He noticed it as a common trait that had been building up inside, waiting for each perfect opportunity to crash to life.

As Franks' day came to an end, a man sat inside his one bedroom apartment, planning a night of self-relievement. He sat crossed-legged in his underwear, holding the sides of his face and determining the process of a well thought out execution. The world was a vast plain of options, and if his options did not prove carnivorous in some way, he felt doomed for a defeat. The man rocked to the beat of his flooding mind. He would not notice it himself, but low, rumbling whimpers constantly escaped his trembling lips.

It was his meaning in life to self-pleasure, but even pleasure comes with a small price of pain. But with a psychotic man, pain does not stay for long. At least, not with the man that began laughing himself into a frenzy in the middle of his living room. No. That man felt little pain. And on this approaching night, it was time for the destruction of innocence. It had to be done. He had waited too long for this since the last relievement. The man laughed until tears formed between his closed lids.

Jason sipped black coffee outside his boss's trailer, checking his watch and making damn sure it was almost clock out time. After he finished his small paper cup, he belched loudly, threw it in the waste bucket beside the trailer entrance and walked inside. His boss was an overweight, balding man who sweated more than your average bear. No matter what temperature the room or outside would be, Dave Former would glisten like a star entering orbit. And his attitude matched his sweat – crude and disgusting. He glanced at Jason for a split second, and returned to his 'paperwork' he somehow could never finish.

"Mr. Former. I was going to ask you..." Dave interrupted him with a heavy sigh, not looking up from his paper. "My daughter has a dance recital tonight, and since I've been so proud of her, I would like to take a day off tomorrow and take her to do something fun." Jason stopped there, waiting for the negative response he was about to get.

"All of the fucking lumber shipped from MONDAY has only been half organized on your side of the keeping. I feel like your work is really dampening day by day. I was willing to let it slide, but now you are asking for a fucking day off tomorrow?" He still did not look up from his 'paperwork', although it was quite obvious he was only staring at them in a poor attempt at avoiding eye contact. "What should I do, Jason? Just let you come and go as you please? What about the other guys? You supposed to be some special case?" Finally, he raised his head to Jason.

Jason rubbed and squeezed his eyes in frustration.

"Do you know what I did before this job, Mr. Former?" His voice was seething with irritation. Dave only flickered his eyes and shrugged his shoulders. "I was a real estate agent, and I absolutely loved it at the time. Helping people with their first start at a family find a home they could begin their life with was true grace for me. But my fucking daughter died, and my fucking wife. I started hating people, all people, every kind. I didn't give a fuck about their happiness because I had none. I hate dealing with people nowadays, especially your condescending ass. I'm taking a fucking day off tomorrow, that will be my first I've taken in two months. It will be fine for you, and fine for me. If not, I guess I won't see you on Monday. Because I've stated and stated on numerous times, I can't work overtime Saturdays in the first place. So, I'll be seeing you Monday." Jason brushed his hair back tightly, holding onto the top of his head and reaching for the exit.

"You better not show up one more fucking time smelling like booze either!" Dave screamed, with the door shutting in front of him before he finished.

Jason's four door Grand Prix was much like his soul these days, cold on the inside. The briskness of the day's dew accumulated through the cracks of the vehicle, creating goosebumps on his flesh. Today was an eventful one, and anxiety could not win this battle. It had won too many battles beforehand. It had become somewhat of an arch rival. It was a foot chase to no end.

*Black rose, left shoulder.*

Before his mind could brace his current reality, the car was already in drive and headed for Maddox's school. She loved to be surprised with an unannounced pick-up, and goddammit he was going to make her happy on this day – if only this day for a while. He knew the stress that coagulated in between the cracks of their relationship.

She hid her pain with a mask, much like anyone, but not in a way a child should. A child who must learn the brutal truth of life at such a young age somehow emerges a different person, with a much higher maturity. It's almost as if adolescence only comes into focus when the reality around them is revealed. It was his job to remind her what it was like to be a child. The rain had tapered off to nothing, leaving only a thickness of moisture in the air. He left the radio off to get himself straight and proper – away from his complexes.

He reached her school fifteen minutes later. Her smile that greeted him outside the double doors was enough to suppress any bad memory, but still it lingered there behind his untold truths. One of the darkest corners of any person's mind. While the sun barely shone, they embraced each other with a compassion long lost and hidden, but every so often found. It was what Jason needed, and he knew

Maddox did too.

They walked back to the car, hand in hand and a lasting smile on their faces. It was turning out to be a good day for both of them. They would arrive home and get ready for Maddox's dance show. Her sense of anticipated triumph held firm in her little hands. She was ready, and so was Jason, to try and start a gratifying new life together. Sometimes, pretending to be happy is better than being engulfed in misery 24/7. Every once in a while, everyone needs a break.

"Daddy! How do I look?!" Maddox swung herself around in an elegant way, which reminded Jason of one of those graceful dancers in White Christmas with Bing Crosby. Her dress fit tight to her slender legs and parachuted out with sparkled cloth that appeared heavenly.

"I think you just may be the most beautiful girl I ever had the pleasure to lay my eyes on," Jason said, holding back the oncoming storm of tears needing to be released. In honesty, she looked like Sage at that age. So full of love and glowing a brilliantly bright light from her eyes alone, she could melt the hearts of just about everyone. Just as

Maddox was about to do in front of an audience.

She leaped into his arms and pulled tight around his neck. He didn't remember a time when she was this loving, and he couldn't remember a time when he was immersively accepting to the feelings around him. Something long dead had awoken inside of him, long forgotten but breathing heavily on its own now.

"I'll change and we can cracka-lack. Sound snazzy?" She answered with another radiant smile and hug; her excitement was contagious. Jason closed his eyes and breathed in, noticing himself how good it felt to be alive again.

John Franks sat in his car outside a liquor store in a small, dilapidated parking lot. He was debating whether or not he was going to enter the store again for the third time to snatch another pint of cheap vodka. Oddly, cheap vodka was the only thing these days that did the trick for John. Anything else just left a bad taste in his mouth, and an ache in his brain.

He flipped open his wallet, glancing at the shining badge briefly, sending a shock of guilt to his bubbling stomach. He was drunk, and feeling sorry for himself, much like his stepfather used to do every single night after work. It's funny how you eventually become the very things you hate. It's as if you concentrate on the hate for that person so intently, your body knows nothing else, and the morphing procedure begins. But it was a trait he got used to. He had to flush the bacteria from his system with poison, it was the only way.

He took his last swig of charcoal water and for a split glimpse, he saw himself pulling his pistol from his holster and placing it to his temple. The last party favor to end all parties. John could not handle the injustice within the system. As killers became free, John Franks became a prisoner. So in turn, a bullet to the skull was the only absolution. Fuck, they might as well write it on his tombstone. He giggled into a laughing fit, still holding the pint sized bottle. His teeth glistened from the bright party store lights outside.

Instead of suicide, John went inside for another pint. Upon entry, the store clerk stared wearily, wondering the drunk man's next move. John stood at the glass doors, somewhat confused at his mission, until the liquor bottles came back into focus. He obtained more of his poison, and drank it to nothing in mere minutes. As Jason gained redemption in small doses, John realized the meaningless existence of his now alcohol fueled life. The paths that were to cross would implode in a series of life changing events. The course had now been set.

If a man did exist as a monster, if a human was born to be evil, it was Kevin Farrand. It wasn't his male cousin sucking his pecker at the age of ten, it wasn't the endless images of death on TV that made him this way; he was born to be the decider of lives. He held the power of life in his hands, and if beauty and innocence held powerful enough, he would decide for them to be victims.

Kevin held his shaking knees outside his bedroom door, bent over and vulnerable. He knew the events about to take place, and his nerves had jumped into overdrive for preparation. After a deep breath to cleanse his being, he decided it was time to begin. In one hour, he would be the murderer of five young girls. The thought sent a euphoric rush of endorphins through his body. He threw a coat on quickly, catching a glimpse of the black rose tattoo on his shoulder. Everything beautiful must die – the perfect metaphor for his destiny.

Jason and Maddox arrived at Rosemary Event Center around 6:45PM, with laughter and jokes filling the car ride there. Jason had lip synched a song on the radio, much to Maddox's enjoyment. Her laughter echoed around Jason's ear, something he needed more than he could have ever imagined in this lifetime. He did not have to look back to his little girl, he could see her in his mind, eyes tearing from the pressure of her laughter – it made him laugh harder.

It continued to be a good night. The last few hours of a relieving night before the plunge to a reality not yet recognized. Her show started at 7:30, and Jason departed from his daughter backstage fifteen minutes before showtime. He sat in the second row, his proudness beaming from him with a permanent smile. He could see her dancing coach, standing on the side of the stage, examining the large crowd in front of him. His sweat shined from the dimly lit stage lights above him.

It was almost 7:30 and the show was about to begin. Jason sat happy, and waited.

John Franks arrived home around 7:20PM, practically to the point of 'blackout drunk'. He tried to focus on his keys, his house, and how the hell he planned on getting inside. His vision multiplied everything times four, and it was a miracle on the grace of God's nutsack he made it home alive. By the time John fell face first on his couch, TV on and softly producing sound, it was 7:45PM. He closed his eyes to thoughts of ending the miserable day behind him. Only, in an imperfect world, it is not always the case. Little did John know, the night was just getting started.

Kevin arrived at the house at 7:32PM. Dusk drew in early as rain clouds overran the sky. His heart thudded like thunder over a long distanced plain. It was just about time to do what he'd been waiting for these past months. Exactly as expected, the parents' car was gone from the driveway. He could see a shadow outside the kitchen, walking past all the low burning lights in the house. He knew who it was – his victim.

He imagined her thighs jiggling with each step to the perfection her walk. *Wouldn't it be nice to carve some of that meat from those exquisite legs? How fucking lovely would those thighs look with blood smeared all over them?*

Kevin decided to wait until 7:45 to make his move; a nice little stakeout before execution was always a thing needed to be done. With adrenaline fueled to the max, Kevin lowered his head, made fists with both hands, and beat himself on top of the head until the throb tipped to a rough numb.

At 7:46PM, a frosted blonde-brunette girl heard a knock at the door. She answered, to a man with a buzzed haircut to his scalp, sweating and panting rapidly. Before a reaction could take course, the man launched his four fingers inside her mouth, gripping her jaw with his thumb pressed under her chin. He threw her with an incomprehensible force, sending her flying backward. Her head smacked the floor with a nasty sound like a dropped melon on linoleum. Blood began to flow instantly, which only fueled the crazed man more. He jumped on top of her, pinning her down by her wrists and giggling madly.

"That fucking beauty you possess, I get to take it!" The man screamed.

Kevin removed his hands from her wrists and grabbed her head, placing his thumbs to the stunned girl's eyes.

"Those beautiful blues go first!"

With the thumbs still placed over her twitching eyes, Kevin pushed with all his might. Blood shot up in spouts of carnage. Now, the girl began to scream. Kevin balled his fist and struck the girl on the forehead twice, knocking her head against the floor, more wet melon sounds crashed through the air. With sudden realization, Kevin whipped backward, noticing the door still ajar. He got up quickly to close it, leaving the girl crying in spurts of screams, her arms flailing in the air, reaching for something not there.

"Time to do what you were born to do, you fucking slut. Time to die."

Kevin dropped himself at her legs and began yanking at her blue sport shorts at the waist. Her pussy revealed little hair, disgusting the man violating her. Like a sinister impulse, the man shoved his index and middle finger inside her, placing his thumb on her landing strip of hair. He pulled her by her cunt to him as he grunted in pain. The young girl let out one last scream before he was back, straddled on top of her. Kevin interlocked his hands together, creating a human sledge hammer, and initiated the killing process.

After the third hit, her skull above her nose cracked open, spilling massive amounts of blood and brain fluid over the top of her face. Her mouth opened with gurgled spurts, now releasing blood from there too. The man smiled at this showcase of defeat, she looked beautiful in all the madness. Exhausted, Kevin rolled over onto his back, breathing heavily. He closed his eyes tightly, soaking up the gloriousness of completing a much needed task.

Now, the most tasking part of it all – the cleanup. Kevin sat up quickly, not letting the relaxation fully set in. Work had to be done. He looked down to his left hand, noticing a rip of his skin tight surgical glove just above his knuckles. That was not a good thing. He thought of his DNA escaping his glove by the second, he panicked and ran for the door- stopping mid-way opening the door ajar and looking back at the girl.

A final cough escaped her, sending strings of blood out like confetti. Against better judgement, he continued out the door. The sun was now only partially present; dusk was almost in full throttle. This was the first killing he had done with the sun still present, and his lack of self-control sickened him. He could have waited until dark, yes, but temptation got the best of him. Within two minutes, the man in the pickup truck was out of sight.

Jason stood with the rest of the crowd in applause. The dark purple lights engulfed the stage as the dancers bowed with proud smiles on their faces. Jason looked around and noticed the smiles in the crowd were brighter – proud parents with risen egos. Maddox spotted her dad at the beginning of the show, and consistently looked to his eyes from the stage, seeking approval as if she was going to get it. But now she continued to smile with the other dancers.

He loved seeing her happy. It was about time for both of them. The instructor with his teenage daughter who also coached stood in front of them with his hands raised. It was one of the last happy moments of the night, but to Jason, it lasted an eternity.

After over five minutes of applause, Jason headed for the exit beside the backstage doors, and waited for his daughter. She came out in a sprint and jumped into his arms yet again.

"Did you love it, Daddy?!" Fresh glitter shining on her forehead, she looked almost porcelain.

"I think that was THE best show I have ever attended. And what a bonus, it features my daughter." He grinned until it spread wider with another hug. Parents stood around them, embracing their little ones in the same fashion. It was a warming environment Jason had not experienced in an extensively long time. There actually was a world outside of darkness, where people really do care and love. It was just as believable as it was unbelievable.

The outside moisture of further rain showers tickled their nerves upon leaving. The sun was replaced by a bright, symbolic moon, arrogantly shining through the dark clouds. It resembled a fantasy world, far away in some unheard of dimension. Maddox held firmly onto Jason's loosely gripped hand and skipped all the way to the car. The past raindrops stood scarce on the windshield; it had not rained in a couple hours. With a quick smile to his daughter in the rearview mirror, Jason threw the Grand Prix into gear and began to drive.

The night was on the cusp of beginning.

Kevin did not return home. He drove recklessly around, frantically pondering all the 'could haves' of the humiliating crash course he had just conducted. It was sloppy and unprofessional to say the least. After planning a task for weeks, you expected yourself to be flawless during the execution. But Kevin was far from professional, and his feelings got in the way, in turn making him sloppy. How had he not noticed that fucking rip in his glove? How could pleasure be the perfect ally to blindness?

Ahead of his truck came Farrand road, a dirt road barely used by the small town's population. He needed to cool off and this was the perfect spot to pull over. With a quick left turn, Kevin was driving 35 MPH, watching the tall corn husks beside him. The road branched slightly to the right, creating the perfect spot to pull over.

After placing the truck in park, Kevin screamed wildly into the quiet cab of the truck, gripping the sides of his head with his finger nails. His ass-end was still halfway in the road, but he didn't care – who the fuck would be along anyway? And if there was, he'd fucking kill them too.

As brightness struck his eyes from above, he looked up to the illuminating moon, entranced. He could see the dark clouds approaching, bringing in the righteous storm they were born to unleash. The thought made him loosen his grip on himself and smile. A morbid portrait of failure could be flung out over Kevin's miserable life, but that never stopped him before. There was great comfort in that.

"I spy something bright green, closer to you than me." Maddox immediately clapped a hand over her mouth in the backseat, to hold in a giggle and to try and imitate a 'poker face'. Jason looked around the car and caught the glow of the car radio; it was 9:03PM.

"The radio. It is the radio!" He screamed it in

a British dictator voice, one of her favorites among many others. But not until now had Jason remembered using that voice, as it had been one of Sage's favorites too. She would beg him to speak it with her friends over as they laughed hysterically.

It also, just now, occurred to Jason this was the first day he could remember where the thought of Sage did not bring him agony. It was a change that came without notice, and he pondered the thought of why. He realized in an ugly manner that he had turned his deceased daughter into his own private nightmare, a source where only negative energy flowed through her. It was a massive transition lost within the horrible events that had occurred to all of them.

The sky lit up bright above them as he drove down Miller Street. He thought about a car ride home he had with Sage after he picked her up from school. She sat where the empty seat beside him was now, her lip protruded in a pout, something she had learned from her mother. Jason had gotten a phone call at work about his daughter smoking in the bathroom. Her principal showed little concern, but expressed a hasty discipline for her when she got home.

Jason thought he would take the Ol' Farrand ghost road his Dad always took him on for conversations. It helped his Dad get through to him, maybe the same principle still worked with a daughter. By the time they reached the end of the road, Sage was happy and Jason felt better too.

"You know, a long time ago, in some realm farthest from Earth, I was once a teenager too. Smoking was invented before me, maybe by a couple months or so." Jason giggled and watched as his daughter barked with laughter at the statement. He connected with her, like a father should. It was one of the last bonds they had together.

Now, as if dreams come to life all too often, Farrand Road approached to the left. Without much thought, Jason flicked his blinker on and made the turn. It was that turn which would set them on the collision course from Hell. Life to some is one big obstacle course, with occasional breaks that build up enough momentum to complete the next obstacle. Only, this was no ordinary obstacle.

John remained passed out, face first in his

pillow with his mouth wide. Spittle formed and pooled around the black stubble on his chin. Being extreme drunk to John was a way to sleep without the nightmares that haunted him. But on this sleep, it was a trance of deep thought. It was not the victims of the lost swarming his mind, it was the other world of regret, one that was suppressed further down than anything else in John.

He thought of the last time he saw his son. The little boy cried with a pathetic whine as he watched his father leave. His mother stood above him with her arms crossed, her stare enough to melt paint off the walls. Memories of pleading to his ex-wife to see him again tore with the soft spots of his brain, ripping them open – spilling more trapped skeletons. His ex-wife's shrill voice demanding him to leave charged deeper, yanking John's eyes open with a forced breath escaping him.

John sprung his head up, blinking rapidly into the darkness. The strong headache knocked him back down on his pillow. This was going to be long night.

The crash ignited in an instant. Jason had taken his eyes off the road for a mere second before it happened. His eyes left the road, going to his daughter in the backseat. She was having a laughing fit after Jason made a joke about how hysterically funny it would be – Jason dancing on a stage in front of a large crowd. He remarked about falling off the stage, and Maddox was struck with intense laughter.

The collision crunched and detracted Jason's car instantly, booming loudly with shattered glass, exploding metal and fiberglass. The other vehicle, a truck, lifted partially, resting the tip of the bed onto Jason's crumpled hood. Smoke billowed with a hiss as the engine died. Jason immediately sprung backward into the backseat to examine Maddox, who was wide eyed and stunned from the commotion. They hit doing forty, but the truck being at a halt already lessened the impact of a moving vehicle. She whined lightly until she was crying.

"You're okay, baby girl, I promise. I am so sorry." Jason felt around her tiny frame for any noticeable injuries and found nothing. She was in shock, but responsive – a very good thing.

The man in the truck grabbed his head while straining his eyes until tears pushed out the ducts. He was having a good laugh before the bullshit. The thought, *at least I didn't ejaculate this time* popped back up in his foggy brain, sending laughing forth once again. What motherfucker rear ends someone parked on the side of the road anyway? He should kill the fucker on principal. The rage from that rumination jerked his arm to the door, flinging it open with a force that brought it right back shut onto him as he began to crawl out.

Jason calmed down Maddox as she coughed over choked up cries. Snot and saliva ran down in strings to her still flawless dance dress. The sparkles on her clothing reflected into Jason's eyes. He looked over his shoulder, and caught a glimpse of a man outside the damaged truck. He spun his head back to his daughter.

"Calm down, honey. You're fine, I promise."

"Daddy! You got blood all over your face!"

Jason touched exactly where the cut formed above the bridge of his nose. His face must have hit the steering wheel upon impact. Adrenaline caused him to systematically put it in the back of his head. Blood ran down his nose, around his mouth, and down his chin in one squiggly river. He looked back to the man who appeared to be removing a jacket, his sight still blurred from the now realized trauma to his head.

"I'm fine, babe. Stay here. Dad is going to check on the other driver. Stay right here."

Jason opened the door quickly, and stood up as if he was a soldier demanded for attention. The man stood by his truck, shadowed by the dark. The only illumination was from his own headlights of the truck that were still on. The man looked pudgy with little to no hair. Jason approached closer, sensing an uneasy feeling from the quiet victim in front of him.

"Are you okay? Your truck, it just came out of nowhere. Are you okay?" Jason tried to sound straightforward but instead sounded shaky, which was the truth. The man remained silent, but continued to move forward also. "Are you able to speak?"

"Yes, I'm able to fuckin' speak. Just kinda pissed, ya know?" The man sounded much softer than his silhouetted figure suggested. "I was just sittin' there one second and the next second – WHAM!" The man clapped his hands together to signify the impact.

"I really am sorry. I didn't see you until it was too late." Of course, that was a lie. Jason had not seen him at all until the collision threw his face into the steering wheel. They walked a couple steps closer to one another. Jason could now see the man's face, red and blotched. His eyes were swollen with past tears. "Are you sure you are okay?"

"Oh yeah. Fuck yeah. I've been through much worse." A giggle escaped the man and his loose stomach jiggled with the vibrations. The laugh crawled under Jason's skin, slithering through his nerves like a snake through long grass.

"O-okay. I'm gonna grab my cellphone. Gotta call the police and check on my daughter. I got the insurance information." Jason began walking back to the car, but the man leaped a couple of steps and grabbed his arm.

"Now sir, we don't need to do all that, do we?" Before Jason could fully turn back around, he saw it blast into his vision. The tattoo that had been gripping his brain since his daughter's death, the very thing that gave him drive most days, was staring him right in his face.

He knew all along what Sage had meant with her last words. She had been smart enough to throw out the only clue she could on her last breath. He knew he would find it. It all led up to this. The feeling left his head and torso, and suddenly he felt lightheaded and dizzy. The tattoo was on his left shoulder, partially hidden under the sleeveless shirt he wore, the head of the rose was coal black, only cracked with age spots.

In response, Jason yanked his arm away from the man's grip, muttering incoherently. "Woah, man. No need to get feisty," the man said, a little surprised at Jason's reaction.

"You-you." Jason could not get words out of his mouth. The chunky man poked a grin as if reading Jason's mind. Jason snarled, spilling spittle down his bloody chin. "You fucking killed her!" Jason whipped his head back to the car and saw Maddox glaring with terrified bug eyes; he ran to her on impulse. The man stood frozen still, trying to grasp what he had just heard. Jason tried opening the car door but could hardly move his fingers. Maddox screamed from the inside. The man gained control again of his focus, and began towards Jason and Maddox.

John could not fall back asleep after his thought escapades had woken him. He went to the bathroom, and gave himself a long look in the mirror while popping four painkillers to ward off the storm inside his head. He could feel his drunkenness slowly dissipating, bringing in the painful sobriety he hated to be awake for. He thought back to his son, and guilt washed through him.

He had not thought of him in days, but the boy always came back like clockwork to remind him of his negligence. *In a perfect world, I would be there for you buddy. In a perfect world, I could do a lot of things for you.* But it was not a perfect world. It was a dreadful world where only the worst scenarios that play inside one's head happen for real. Nightmares and reality go hand in hand; it's fantasy to be able to see the line, because there was no line.

John went to the fridge for much needed relief but only found a partially drank bottle of beer, which would have to suffice. It was amazing how little someone could feel after a bad day. It was like all of his failures triggered after one enormously major one. He figured that is how it starts with someone succumbing to depression, until every day is a failure. After downing the opened beer in the refrigerator, his headache took two much needed steps backward. He decided to watch TV to fall back asleep. Soon, a phone call would leave him fully awake.

Jason finally got the car door open and bent inside to a crying Maddox, while snatching the cellphone off of the divider beside the driver's seat. Before Jason could utter a syllable, Maddox's eyes popped with terror at what was coming behind her Dad.

"Dad, the man!" Before Jason could swing his head around, he was charged with tremendous force, catapulting him sideways and onto his back, smacking his head on the car's back tire. Maddox shrieked and yelled as the man hovered above her father.

"Now, what was that you were saying?" the chubby man asked, panting, with a grisly grin still gleaming on his face. Jason launched back to his feet quicker than he left them. He launched himself forward with his head down, catching the man in his squishy belly and knocking him to the ground. Jason held on to the man's waist, until the bulbous killer's head met the concrete as he crashed onto his back. He grabbed the man by the throat and squeezed.

"You killed my daughter, you motherfucker!" Jason's clenched teeth did not part, his words spurting out with spit between his teeth. The man below Jason grunted for air while flailing his arms in wacky positions; his eyes bulged with the pressure, turning his face to grape purple. The man felt the asphalt for something redeeming and found just what he needed.

Jason could see the life slowly leaving the fuck's protruding eyes. The sheer adrenaline in Jason prevented him from seeing or hearing anything else, it was fully bloodlust instinct now in effect. Maddox screamed at the car window beside them as she watched her father's animalistic behavior. The man swung his left hand, and smashed Jason on the side of the head with a rock. Jason lost vision and toppled onto the gasping man, who did not have the energy or power to lift him off.

Through the blackness, Jason swam towards a

shimmer of light. It did not stay still, but shifted with the glare of his eyes, like trying to pinpoint a black dot through thousands of broken blood vessels. In the strands of light that seeped through, the black rose appeared in between the cracks of darkness. His eyes captured the reality around him as the blackness crept away like the opposite effect of a burnt reel. His head bobbed up and down with the labored breathing as his head rested on the man's sweaty chest.

Instinct drove into Jason's soul once again, and his fists turned to hardened balls. Jason quickly rose over Kevin with his left fist raised in a 'hammer down' position. Before Jason could land the bludgeon, the man sprung his straightened fingers forward and struck Jason in the throat, sending him off fiercely. He clenched his throat as air escaped in a hurry, his only thought was to go to Maddox beside him, who was clawing at the window and screaming ferociously.

Jason motioned for her to back away from the window, barely able to remove his hands from his heaving throat. He could not breathe and it only tightened worse after every attempted breath. Jason slammed his shoulder against the window; Maddox screamed and scrambled back across the seat. Her cheeks were flushed and swollen, she looked pitiful but remained gorgeous.

The window cracked slightly toward the top of the glass. Jason flew himself against it once more, this time shattering it upon impact. A shard of glass punctured his left ear, tearing his earlobe where it connected to his face. Blood spilled down his neck as his breath powered through to words.

"Grab my hand, Maddox!" His voice sounded coarse and strained, as if it was coated in sand. Maddox took his hand and he dragged her out of the broken window, knocking down any remaining glass with his own arm before her small body passed through. The man still lay on the ground, but now perched himself up on one elbow. Wounded and foggy, Jason swung his right knee upward into the man's face, flicking his head back with a grunt and a spurt of blood. Jason fell to one knee but quickly reinstated himself.

"Come on, Maddox, we gotta go!" He grabbed his daughter by her trembling hand and made way for the corn field beside them. The tall corn husks swallowed them instantly, leaving the dazed Kevin behind.

The further they voyaged within, the quieter the night became, with only crickets audible through the brisk air. The moon stayed prominent among the coming rain clouds, casting a light for their narrow escape. Jason stopped and fumbled for his phone in his pocket; it displayed only one bar of service, but that was enough to attempt a phone call. He dialed the first person he knew could somehow help him. Fuck 911 in the sense of sending out a couple of "beat cops". He had a chance to end all of this once and for all.

He regretted not continually pummeling the man while he was down, but fear for Maddox got the best of him. He needed to get her someplace safe. His head throbbed from the rock that struck him. He could feel the right side of his face swell and pulse with the amplified surfaced blood. With his bloodied hand he reached for his torn earlobe. It hung from his ear like a morbid tree ornament. Maddox cried harder from the sight.

"I know it looks bad. But it's not. Really." Trying to sound convincing on a night like this was rather difficult as he had no idea how this fucked up event would end. But Maddox's eyes cheered a bit from the reassurance, and she even mustered a slight grin to go with it. Jason admired her undying courage, now all he needed to do was follow suit. Courage was one of the only things getting him and his daughter out alive on this night.

Above them, like a flick of a switch, the rain began once more.

John Franks stayed in a sleep purgatory. Half of him could still see the glare of the infomercials on the TV set, while another part of him remained suspended in a dream-like stupor, plagued with past haunts. The headache had since subsided, but John still felt like shit. It was the perfect punishment for jackass behavior. As the infomercial came to an end, leaving the TV a blank screen, his cellphone erupted into vibration on the coffee table beside him. After realizing with dull enthusiasm that it was not a dream he was hearing, John sat up roughly, his hair stuck up sideways with charged static.

It was Jason Desmoines. Go fucking figure. The perfect end to a failed fucking day. John rubbed his eyes and clicked the 'fuck off' button on his phone. Not today. He would try to sedate himself further with possible liquor options around the house. Only, the phone began buzzing again immediately after the first.

Jason was one persistent son of a bitch, but he usually never called twice in a row, especially at night. John embraced his guilt for being a shit detective, but what kind of detective would he be if he went completely insane? Which was what would eventually happen if he didn't keep some kind of boundary.

The phone ignited a third time. John could not take his eyes off of it as it rotated almost full circle. Before the voicemail could pick it up once again, John lifted it up off of the table and to his ear.

"Jason, listen. I'm not-"

"John, shut the fuck up and listen. I got him." John could hear rain in the background, he sounded like he was standing in the middle of it. It prompted him to walk to his living room window. The rain was coming down steadily. Jason's voice was rough and smeared with anxiety.

"You got him? What are you talk-"

"I got into a fucking car accident. He came after-" The signal was weak and Jason's tone became robotic and filled with static.

"You're cutting the fuck out. What's going on? Where are you?" John tried to mask his irritability with concern, but it was not working in the slightest.

"He killed my daughter, John. It's him."

"Where are you?!" John was gradually slipping over to the side of genuine concern.

"Farrand Road. I'm in a field of corn. I have Maddox with-"

The phone cut out abruptly.

John held the phone firmly to his head, hypnotized with possible scenarios of what could be happening. The poor fucker might have finally snapped, created some kind of altered reality where he was playing some type of fucking Sherlock Holmes. Only, the straight forwardness of his voice was damn right convincing.

He would go and check it out. He was still a goddamn cop after all. It was his job.

Jason threw the phone to the ground, not fully realizing the puddle forming around his boots. The cell splashed with a *thunk* and disappeared in the mud hole. Maddox's crying picked up a couple octaves until it was a shriek. They were both soaked, and the rain had no intentions of giving up. He pulled off his sweater, wrapped it around her, and pulled her tight against him. His white t-shirt saturated immediately and stuck to his body like a second layer of skin.

With a sudden boom of distant thunder, Jason heard rustling corn husks behind them.

"I need you to be brave, okay? Daddy will not let anything happen to you. Daddy will not fail again, ya understand?"

More rustles picked up from heavy foot falls; the man was only a couple feet away. Instead of running, Jason stretched his legs out until he was in his fullest upward position. Without warning, he sprinted toward the breaking husks. The husks slapped his face as Jason pushed forward and the approaching sound stopped, but Jason knew exactly where he was.

With his daughter's protests faintly in the background, he tackled the man blindly. A sharp and piercing pain erupted in his abdomen area, as they both slid through the wet mud. The man groaned, hitting the dirt hard, a broken bottle that was clenched in his hand released and disappeared. Jason leaped to his feet again, with his fists balled, but the man's sneaker connected directly with his left knee. He screamed in pain, and held his leg before collapsing. If there was an audience, it would have been picture perfect for the chubby guy.

Kevin's mind filled with anger at this fucked up act of defiance. He slowly walked to Jason, puffing his breath out as the rain pounded their skin in fierce droplets. His thinning hair folding in thick strands around his forehead. Jason looked up, his lips quivering over his clenched teeth.

"Come on, you motherfucker! Do something!" Jason screamed, still holding his bum knee.

"You should have just let it go. Now I'm going to kill your other girl too."

The magic of adrenaline has been a mystery to

scientists around the world – cases of people lifting cars off of themselves in a fit of panic or rage and more. Survival isn't always a choice we make, sometimes it just engages spontaneously.

Like gas on a dwindling fire, Jason sprung back upon his feet, and swung a right hook at Kevin, connecting him in the jaw. His head snapped to the side with a gasp, taking him by blunt surprise. Jason saw only a red rim around complete blackness, a rage unlike any other.

He brought Kevin back down to the ground with a tackle, and began to pummel him with left and right blows to the face. Kevin did the best he could to block, but was only able to deflect a couple. He reached for the broken bottle once more that lay inches from his head; Jason's blind rage prohibited him from seeing it. Kevin plunged the bottle forward, sticking it into his exposed ribs.

With another scream from Jason, they were beside each other on the puddled ground again, his white shirt now a dark red. Without hesitation, Jason ripped the bottle from his ribs, ejecting blood and chunks of flesh, and swiped Kevin's face with it.

Kevin covered his face as blood slipped through his fingers, yelling incoherent words to the sky.

Maddox's screams now seemed entirely too close and as Jason looked up, blinded by rage and the consistent rain, he saw her right above him. He pulled himself up with his right hand and held his ribs with the other. With a bum leg, he moved with a limp. Maddox gripped his hand, and as Kevin yelped into the sky, the two of them ventured deeper into the corn where eventually, they came to an abandoned barn.

Thankfully to John, Farrand Road was not far away from his home. Dazed and still drunk, John could barely see the road in a whirlwind of rain descending from above. He decided on not calling back-up, it was the least he could do if it was what he thought it was. Jason was just most likely having a meltdown – it happens. Why cause a huge fuss when he could just take care of it himself?

Farrand Road approached on the right, John didn't bother using his blinker and made a sharp turn. The thoughts of his son returned to the black matter of his mind, waiting to make an appearance again when the time was right. Before he could think of anything else, the two cars appeared on the left. There had been an accident after all. He brought the car to an abrupt halt and launched out without closing the door.

No one seemed to be around, except for faint shouting within the corn. Jason's back window was smashed out, telling him something more than an accident had taken place. John went back to his car, gripped his hand gun, and began for the corn.

Jason pushed the barn door open with his free hand as Maddox stood closely behind him. The tall, wooden door opened with a loud creak while the sounds of disturbed bats fluttered above them. Jason was losing blood fast, and his vision kept going from clear to fucked.

"Come on, honey," Jason said, now holding his stomach with both arms. "Let's take some shelter before we freeze to death. Someone will come." He had high hopes for John making an appearance. He had to have believed him, but who was to say since the phone cut out?

Maddox followed him inside and Jason closed the door behind them.

John held his gun out in front of him as he heard noises a few feet ahead. His issued Beretta glistened from the wetness and the giant moon above. The yelling had stopped, and the silence was nerve racking.

"Anyone out here!" he yelled into the dark. A corn husk whipped against his temple and John almost unloaded his clip. "I know someone is out here! This is Detective Franks! I wanna hear some noise from you!" Nothing. Even the rustling he heard previously had ceased. John dunked his foot into a deep puddle and lowered his weapon. He sighed and bent down, not realizing a man standing behind him.

As soon as John heard the squish of approaching foot falls, it was too late. Kevin went for his pistol, but John held firm and they tumbled together into the mud, wrestling over the 9MM. Kevin's face was ripped open sideways from his right eye to the left side of his chin, his right eye now only a bloody milky white. Amongst the panic, John saw the tattoo on the man's left shoulder. It shined bright upon the moistened skin.

The gun flew from both their grips in the hand

strength match. The man seized John by the throat and squeezed, letting out a maniacal scream. John lunged his fists against the man's stomach, but the grip did not loosen.

Somewhere far off in the distance, lightning flashed brightly and thunder rumbled loudly.

Jason sat leaning against the wooden wall of the barn, and Maddox nestled quickly next to him. He mustered strength and threw his left arm around her.

"It will be okay now," Jason said, catching every bit of breath he had. "We'll wait for help to come. We will be okay now." A part of him knew the lie behind this, somehow as a morbid epiphany. He knew the maniac fuck was still alive out there, and suddenly he had doubts about John's arrival.

Maddox only responded with a low whimper. The night's events proved to be too much on her fragile mind, but as she always was, she remained strong. She reached her hand to the bloodied wounds on her father. Jason winced and pulled back.

"Ah. No, don't touch it, I'll be fine." He looked down and took a glimpse at the massacre done to his ribs. The white shirt stuck to the flesh wound fiercely, but ripped cloth revealed deep lacerations and missing chunks of skin. And now, he saw why the sharp pain had been inflicted on his stomach during the initiation of the scuffle. He was stabbed twice by the broken bottle, his abdomen the reason for the massively erupting blood loss. It was his vision and thinking that was being affected the most.

"Dad. You're hurt bad. You're hurt bad!" She raised her voice to a high pitch that echoed through the abandoned barn with acoustic force.

"I'm fine. Keep your voice down, sweetie. It looks worse than it is." It was another lie he felt he had told her. He could feel his body weaken by the minute.

Together, they huddled and listened to the rain smash against the wooden barn.

John managed to impact with enough force onto the man's stomach to let go of his throat. John flipped himself on top of the man and jammed his thumb into the already obliterated eyeball. He screamed in pain, and launched a fist into John's temple, knocking him semi-unconscious.

Kevin rose up, injured and maddened. John

saw him towering above, the lightning exposing his lunatic expression of carnage. The man lifted his right foot and dropped it down on John's skull. He was not satisfied with one stomp, so he tried two, which succeeded with a crunch. The detective turned his head to the side slowly, and ceased movement. Kevin glared at him for a long while, and began further into the corn. That asshole and his daughter had to be out there somewhere, and he was going to find them. His freedom depended on it.

Jason and Maddox huddled until they were just about to fall asleep. They both heard a screeching scream from afar. Jason knew immediately what it had to be. Detective Franks arrived and was taking care of the problem. Something Jason couldn't do, not even to the person who brutally murdered his daughter.

"Dad? What was that? He's coming for us again, isn't he? He's going to kill us!" Jason grabbed the back of her head and put it to his chest to cradle her.

"Stay quiet. It will all be over soon."

The rain sounded like a jet engine preparing

for take off outside, the old wood of the barn vibrating as each droplet forcefully hit. It reminded Jason of a time with Sage. It had been a Thursday, and Sage's soccer game was about to commence. It was a big week for her, as the team they were facing was top ten – it would take a lot of endurance for a team victory.

Sage was fourteen. He could still see her in her uniform, hair put up in a bun and socks pulled up to her knees. As if by some freak of nature intervention, rain downpoured right before kick off. While on their way home from the cancelled game, the rain had gotten so heavy Jason had to pull the car over.

"Well, either God didn't want you guys to lose or He had to take a massive piss, either way, this is intense and I cannot see for shit." His wife and daughter bellowed out with laughter until tears poured down their faces. And that's how they spent the time on the side of the road, cracking jokes and enjoying life. It was the little things that kept the family going, even upon disappointment.

Jason's vision blurred as his thoughts trained

his eyes to the leaking roof of the barn. He had almost forgotten about the scream, and wished he had enough energy in him to check on the situation. Maddox was silent; he looked down to see she had fallen asleep. Jason shifted slowly, trying not to wake her. The big, wooden barn door shook mildly, with a creak that shifted through the air and the sound of the rain.

Jason removed Maddox from him and propped her against the wall; she sighed softly, but her eyes remained shut. He hobbled to the door, bracing the ground with his left hand with each step. It was upon this, Jason realized exactly how bad of condition he actually was in.

The door swung leisurely ajar. Jason held his breath and waited for the man to burst through, with hopes that it would be John. Only the killer appeared, lightning flashing behind him. The wind blew his little amount of hair sideways in a dynamic breeze. He resembled a slasher from a 70's Grindhouse film. Jason tried standing upright to confront him, but his injury forced him to slump.

"I fucking told you to let be, guy. Now I'm

going to kill you and that little bitch of yours once and for all. I mean face it, what choice do I have? You know my dirty little secret. Besides, you guys aren't exactly my taste."

Jason screamed as loud as his vocal chords would allow and hurtled forward with his shoulder down, the best way to bring the big guy down. However, Kevin met Jason's shoulder with his own and they clashed with a loud crack. Jason sprung backward, sliding against the barn. Kevin dove on top, and jammed his four fingers into Jason's abdomen wound.

The pain went immediately numb, rendering Jason free of any sensation. Blood oozed around the man's fat fingers. Jason saw the only open body part he could reach. He opened his mouth, gripped it around Kevin's nose, and clenched his teeth, feeling the man's skin slice apart with the force.

The metallic tasting fluid poured down Jason's throat and into his esophagus, choking him up and forcing him to let go as the man screamed with his fingers inside Jason's stomach. Jason managed to get a hand free and brought it forward into Kevin's mutilated nose. It snapped sideways at the part of bite wound. Finally, the man flopped backward, coughing and panting. Jason gagged and vomited while climbing back to his feet.

At the edge of the corn, he saw his daughter Sage. Her dress was pink, and shined in the moonlight. There had not been a spot on her. He glimpsed her falling, crashing to linoleum; her head smacked the floor with a wet splat. He saw the blood that formed around her head.

Black rose, left shoulder...

Over the frightened, struggling girl, the man before him was looking deep into her pleading eyes. She begged but in the end, he showed no mercy.

His daughter vanished until all he was staring at was the field. But to the right, like a gleaming diamond, a rusted pitchfork lay on the ground, hidden partially by a haystack. Jason sprinted to the best of his abilities toward it. He hooked his hands around the weapon and whipped back toward the man. He was not there. The barn door moved back and forth with the rhythm of the wind. Jason burst with panic and forced his knee to work properly.

"Maddox! Don't you fucking touch her, you motherfucker, I'll kill you!" He reached the doorway and saw the man running. Maddox screamed and jolted into the opposite direction. "Stay away from her!" Jason could barely screech, his throat dried thick with mucus.

Kevin stopped in his tracks and turned around. Jason met his eyes, his pitch fork held out in front. "Why did you push me this far? Are you mad I killed your daughter? You're not over that by now?"

"No father could, you sonofabitch, I'm going to end this right now."

Kevin turned back around and sprinted toward Maddox, who was climbing frantically up a ladder built into the side of the barn and leading up to a small loft. Maddox reached the wooden platform and proceeded to pull herself up. Kevin reached the ladder and stopped, while looking up at Maddox as she peeked her small head over the edge.

"Sorry, little girl. Your father brought this on you..."

While placing one hand on the ladder, his foot did not reach the rung. Jason plunged the pitchfork into the back of the man's neck. One of the prongs penetrated straight through, spilling blood in a gushing fountain. Jason ripped the pitchfork back, leaving the hole and an easy escape route for Kevin's blood. He gurgled while turning around to Jason, plucking at the wound as it continued to pour out. Jason plunged it forward once more, penetrating all six prongs to the man's chest. Kevin spat up dark chunks of blood as his breath was mostly escaping his throat. He dropped down to his knees, with eyes now begging for mercy he would not receive.

"Daddy! Here!" Maddox dropped down a framing hammer. It landed in front of Kevin while his breath slowed with small spurts of blood from his chest. He sounded like an astronaut with no oxygen in his vessel. Jason picked up the hammer and without hesitation, drove the claw end into Kevin's forehead. The hammer ripped down on his skull, tearing the front of his face outward. He fell forward with his brain partially exposed. It leaked like a broken fire hydrant. After a few brief, violent twitches, the man lay completely still.

Jason looked up at his daughter and smiled, before falling backward with a loud thud as his body hit the ground.

John woke up, half expecting to be half-drunk, in bed, with a jolting headache. Well, he got the headache part excruciatingly correct. Thick mud was caked onto his previous day's white dress shirt, with a mixture of blood. He could not move his jaw, and it appeared he was lying in the middle of a field.

He slowly tried to rise up, but could only sit due to the pain in his knees. He bent forward and panted heavily. The left side of his face felt like fire, and he could feel the puffiness of the swelling pulsating through his temples. He put his left foot to the ground and made an attempt at standing, eventually making it successfully to both feet.

The rain had died down to a low sprinkle and the dark clouds above began to scatter to a dull black. The moon glowed prominently, still giving light to this fucked up show of carnage. John stood in the moonlight, frozen, trying to recollect the events that had just transpired. By instinct, he headed deeper into the tall field.

Fifteen minutes later, he reached the abandoned barn. His walk was slow and clumsy; he had fallen numerous times, but always got back up with a steady quickness. He approached the barn with caution; the door was slightly ajar and lightly blowing in the wind. He heard the little girl crying first, and ran toward the sound. The barn was dark inside, except for the light of the moon shining through the cracks in the walls and roof.

At the far end of the barn was a small girl sobbing, with a man's head propped upon her lap. It was Jason Desmoines, and his little daughter, Maddox. Jason's eyes were partially open, and tears streamed down his dirtied face. Next to them was a body – the man who had attacked John. John could not talk, so he sat beside them and placed his hand on Jason's face.

"We got him," Jason whispered. "We finally put an end to it all."

Jason's eyes closed, for the last time.

A woman sat in front of her computer screen, gazing at the unfinished report she had to complete by the day's end. Her small cubicle was cluttered with pictures of her past, mostly her father. She was daydreaming of the last good time she had with her dad. The way they had laughed together before the long plunge into a very different life.

After her father died, the police detective who presided over her family's case took her in and treated her as his own. In the adventure, Maddox had gained a stepbrother who she had learned to love more than she ever thought possible. It was a chain reaction of events to no end, but somehow, it did. It ended with somewhat of a happy ending also, something she thought was inconceivable.

"You gonna have those done today?" A gawky, pale man stood above her, gripping a coffee mug as if it were a life support system. Sweat beaded off of his long forehead. "We can't fall behind, remember?"

Maddox broke her stare from the screen and looked back at the tall man behind her. She hadn't registered any of his words, so she confirmed with a slight smile. The man nodded and walked on his way.

The years after her father's death were no easy task; in fact, it was more of a test of strength. She thought at one time that she could not possibly feel anything worse than losing her big sister and mother, only to be sadly mistaken the night her father was taken from her. But his life was not in vain, and the monster had finally been slain.

Long nights by herself, she would think about all the potential lives that had been saved that night, after ending the plague of terror that would have continued for years and years to come. It was all a giant puzzle that was always meant to be placed together, to receive the full picture. The full picture of life after tragedy and death. A picture of hope that few humans ever witness in a single lifetime. Sometimes evil must exist to show us the lessons in life we so often forget.

It happened fifteen years ago.

The fender bender had not been an accident amongst cars. The fender bender had been an accident of dueling lives, colliding to a supernova of consequences.

Maddox sighed in a deep breath and tried to clear her thoughts. She had a report to finish.

# Remember, Satan Loves You

He spotted the dead lady on a Tuesday morning, crouched in the corner of the kitchen. She was wearing a white night gown, covered in a black goo that smelt of burning sulfur. She was clawing at her face while making a weird, screeching moan.

Timothy stood watching her in more amusement than shock. He had felt her presence around before, so it was no surprise to him when she appeared. He took a couple steps toward her as their eyes connected.

"What are you doing here? What do you want?" His voice was small but purposeful.

She replied with another moan of despair. Her eyes watered and more black goo ejected slowly from her mouth, staining her nightgown even further. Timothy stepped backward and sighed.

"You're useless, aren't you? I guess I can't help you." He turned around to walk away.

"Remember, Satan loves you." The voice was clear and somewhat powerful.

Timothy whipped around and found the woman had disappeared.

Molly was late for work, and the traffic jam she was stuck in was not helping anything. She was late getting her son Timothy on the bus, and it was all downhill from there. Rushing inside the gas station to grab a coffee did not end well either, spilling the hot beverage onto her blouse while getting on the expressway.

Now she was stuck in traffic, the rushing before had been pointless. The topping on the cake. Annoyed, she flicked through the radio stations with no luck on anything worth listening to. The cars around her moved occasionally, a couple of feet every couple of minutes – it was a bad jam.

"I bet it's a fuckin' car accident," Molly said to herself. She glanced at her purse just in time to see her phone buzzing off. She answered it immediately.

"Hello, I'm busy, this better be good." She did not recognize the number.

"This is Principal Heyman. I need you to come in immediately." His voice was stern and forceful. It was definitely something important.

"What? Why? Is Tim okay?" Her voice was now bleeding with desperation.

"Please, just come in as soon as possible. We may be sending your son home. He drew some disturbing pictures and words. This is not taken lightly here at Mott Elementary, this is very serious. And to make matters worse, he is not being cooperative. A kid at the age of twelve needs to have proper respect for authority."

"I'll be there when I can. Stuck in traffic at the moment. And I don't appreciate you scorning my parenting skills over the phone."

"See you soon," he curtly replied, and hung up.

Molly grabbed a cigarette and aggressively lit it. It was not turning out to be a good day at all.

The Principal was standing outside his office door when she arrived. She could see Timothy inside his office through the solid plate glass.

"So, why the Hell am I here?" Molly said, throwing her hands in the air.

"Well, I will show you." He shifted his head toward the office and they both walked in. Timothy was sitting in the chair with his arms crossed, sulking. Molly walked over to him and gently placed her arm on his bent forward neck as his head remained down. Mr. Heyman hurried to his seat and reached for two papers sitting on his desk. He held them out to Molly, who snatched the papers rudely.

The first paper was nothing but words. The same words over and over again. SATIN LOVES YOU, SATIN LOVES YOU, SATIN LOVES YOU. It was written from top to bottom. She knew what the word was supposed to be: SATAN. The other paper had a drawn picture of a woman, colored in completely black. She was lying down with blood scribbled violently around her body. It was crude and sloppy, yet had a tone of realism between the lines of the image.

Molly lowered the papers from her face and glanced down at Timothy before engaging with Mr. Heyman.

"Yes well, he has an overactive imagination. Sometimes that's considered a good thing, ya know. Imagination is better than being dull, right?" She wanted to sound convincing, but the pictures were in fact disturbing, even to her. As of matter of fact, they scared her. She did not want to look at them again.

"Mrs. Tameran, I-"

"Miss, I am a miss," Molly corrected sternly.

"Ms. Tameran," Mr. Heyman said with a smirk that expressed how her rudeness was not whatsoever bothersome. "These pictures are not appropriate for anywhere, especially school. We have a code and rules to follow. At the age of twelve, he should know better than to think something of that manner would be acceptable." He looked to Timothy. "Don't you think you should have known better?"

"Don't belittle him like that! He's a kid! He probably dreamed of it and wanted to express himself about it! How dare this be made into such a fuss!" The entire situation made her uneasy, and in turn she resorted to justifications. It was her one and only defense mechanism.

"Ms. Tameran, it made his teacher Ms. Halloway uncomfortable. I think the rest of the day off for him is suitable. Let the air thin a bit." With this, he sat down in his chair behind his desk. He resembled an overworked car salesman losing hope on a good sale.

"Well, whatever makes your job easier. I guess that will have to do. And thank you for making me miss work over something so incredibly futile." Timothy looked up to his mother as she waved her hand to get him moving.

Timothy sat in the back seat and remained quiet until Molly finally broke the ice. It reminded her of his father, who seemed to solve everything through silence. At one point in time, months before his death, he kept silent for over a week to Molly. She forgot what the dilemma had been, but it was always something trivial. Not even alcohol could get the man to talk. If he was bothered, his lips became sealed.

"So, Tim. What made you want to write that? And draw those pictures?" She glanced back and forth from the road to him through the rearview mirror.

Timothy stared blankly at her reflection before finally shrugging his shoulders. Molly sighed and pressed again.

"Did you just think of that in your head? Do you even know who Satan is?"

Another shrug.

"You know your father used to give me the same silent treatment. But eventually, no matter how long it may be, he always eventually opened up." She thought possibly the mention of his father would initiate a response, but it did not. They drove in silence until they reached the two car driveway of their home. He blurted the sentence out as if it forcefully spewed on impulse.

"I think he loves me, you know." His eyes grew large as if he himself was surprised by his statement. Without letting his mom respond, he exited the car and headed for the front door.

Dinner was filled with more awkward silence. Timothy ate his roast beef slowly, not once looking up from his picked at plate. He looked like his father, and memories of him flooded her mind, expelling scenario after scenario of times when he had acted the exact same way. It saddened her greatly, and the thought of her son not being able to confide in her bugged and probed the sensitivity code in her brain. She couldn't help the anger impatiently waiting behind her heart. It knocked at the door, ready to be let out.

"If you have nothing to say to me, then I guess you've had enough dinner." She stabbed into her roast beef while scowling at her son. He had to know that boundaries were always set, and he was treading over the line with her patience.

Timothy looked up at her, surprised at his mother's sternness. He dropped his fork onto his plate and stood up. His eyes transferred from bewilderment to annoyance.

"Mom, there are things you should not know about. Things that I don't even know about. I don't have to talk to you if I don't wanna." He shoved his chair in forcefully and stomped to his bedroom. His mother had no reply for him.

Molly slowly finished her plate in the quiet, pondering the words of her troubled son. It was the look in his eyes which made the biggest impact on it all. She had never seen such deep emotion behind his tiny blues. There was a story within them, screaming to get out. But she did not know the story, as much as she would like to. It was as much of a mystery as everything with his recent behavior.

The phone rang loudly to her left, throwing her from her thoughts and back to existence. It was the house phone, braced against the wall by the bay window. Without reasoning why, she ran to it frantically.

"Hello, yeah." Her breath stressed in long puffs of air.

Only a dial tone answered back.

Timothy lay in bed, staring at the ceiling as shadows from the outside trees danced into different diabolical shapes. It upset him his mother would rather get mad than to understand the changes that were happening. Sure, she didn't know (nor did he, but he felt it), but as his mother, she should at least have the decency to respect it. In all truthfulness, he had not meant to draw that picture or write those words. It just happened on its own. Like disassociation writing, only more vivid and powerful.

He heard the rustling under his bed and knew it was another visitor. Hopefully this time, the thing will be more insightful. Timothy did not break his gaze at the shadows, only listened as the thing under him moved with a moist-slimy, slithering sound.

"Tim. Tim, I'm over here. I need to see you." The voice was rough and scratchy, but child-like also.

"What is it you come for?" His gaze remained intact. He noticed the shadows now dancing more viciously. The shapes became bolder; a set of thick horns drifted leisurely across his paste white ceiling, starting from the window up.

"I need to see you. You can trust in me, Timmy. I promise."

Timothy leaped sideways with his eyes full as saucers. "Don't call me Timmy!"

Timothy met the dead boy immediately. Without realizing, he gasped upon first view. The dead boy below him had no arms or legs, and was naked; slithering on his torso from the wetness of his leaking blood. The dark red oozed from the severed nubs, while also escaping in random streams from his mouth. His eyes were black and sunken, and the skin on his face was partially decomposed. A shiny gleam of silver light glistened from the corpse's right eye under a torn eyelid that hung to the side. It smiled at the lash out.

"So sorry for the apparent insult. That is the

last thing we would want to do." It slinked like a serpent in tall grass, the boy's upper torso rested onto Tim's bed as it rose up – their faces inches apart. Timothy could smell the rot of damnation radiating from the skin. The black eyes ignited yellow flames deep behind the glassy balls. The moon's light shined upon its face. The boy was around the same age.

"What is it you all want with me? What am I supposed to do?" Timothy closed his eyes and looked to his lap as he sat up against the headboard of his bed. "I feel like there is something for me to do. Something to prove."

It threw its head back and bellowed laughter. "You're exactly right! Proof is in the flesh, but loyalty you must initiate."

"I can be loyal." Timothy crossed his arms and presented a 'tough guy' expression. "I can be anything you all want me to be."

"That's what I said, and I couldn't be happier. You will know when. You will know when the time is." Blood escaped the boy's dried lips onto the bed sheets. It smiled and giggled as more blood oozed between its teeth. The tone was not of a boy any longer. It was a very old man, and Tim could have sworn the face grew old along with it. "You will feel it within you."

The dead boy flopped down to the hardwood floor and slithered back underneath the bed. The trail of blood was still fresh behind it and shining in the faded light of the moon above. Its voice diminished with it.

"Be with us. Remember, Satan loves you. Always."

Timothy jumped up from his bed and looked around his room. It was now completely quiet again, with only the faint sound of his mother in the living room downstairs. He had to use the bathroom, but resisted the urge as his mom was still awake. He did not feel like being bombarded with an endless line of questions. Instead, he decided to try and get some sleep. He had a lot to prepare for, but had no idea what.

"Now, you know what's suitable and what isn't, I reckon?" Ms. Halloway had her small hand on his shoulder. She was young, and the doubt lit up the greenness of her eyes, making her look twice her age.

Her long blonde hair was sloppily placed in a bun behind her head. She looked unrested compared to the day prior.

"Yes." Timothy looked to his sneakers and walked with his head down to his desk. She stood at the center of the class and waited for everyone to be seated.

"Today, we're going to be doing a lot of reading. It appears I've caught some sort of bug and don't feel very pleasant. I think a day of catching up in the books will suffice." She hesitated while looking around the classroom. The students remained quiet.

Timothy opened up a comic book he brought from home that showcased Van Helsing swarmed by bloodthirsty vampires. It was one of his favorites. But today, the pictures somehow looked different. The illustrations far more bloody than he had ever remembered them to be. He smiled and took it in as a gift from the ones who visit him.

On page five, a woman beheaded lay in a pool of blood in front of an old, Victorian style castle. The woman cast a high resemblance to his teacher Ms. Halloway, down to her flower plagued blouse and black dress pants. Timothy looked up from the book, catching Ms. Halloway in deep concentration, eyes fixed on him. It took him aback and jolted his body backward. His desk screeched through the silence of the classroom.

The woman's stare did not break until she stood up and looked to the back of the room. Timothy turned his head behind him and saw the man she had been looking at. He wore nothing except for torn cloth that covered his genitals. His skin was etched in scars and dirt, and behind him two large, black feathered wings. His eyes were the same black as the boy and woman from home.

Ms. Halloway walked over to a table that rested against her desk, on it, a paper cutter with the blade partially risen up.

"Boys and girls. I would just like to wish everyone the utmost of misery in this diseased cesspool of a world. Damnation among us all." She turned her head to Timothy. "And remember Tim, Satan loves you."

Ms. Halloway rested her head underneath the blade, and with her right hand, she gripped the handle of it. The children around the classroom sat frozen in disbelief as the teacher began slamming the blade up and down on her neck. Blood reached the chalkboard in squirts as the sharpened steel ripped through more and more of her flesh. The once quiet room filled with screams from all of the children. All of the children except Timothy, who remained seated, watching with a grin.

After the fourth whack, Ms. Halloway's head became fully removed. It rolled off of the table and fell to the ground, smacking the cold floor like a wet soccer ball. Her headless body stood upright and walked to the chalkboard in a blind-drunken jot. Her arms flailed out in front of her as a sense of vision. She stuck her shaking hand into her wound and wrote slowly in blood SATIN LOVES YOU onto the dusty board before falling into a pool of plasma and twitching viciously.

The children continued to scream until Ms. Halloway became perfectly still. It wasn't until Mr. Richards from across the hall heard all of the commotion and decided to check it out, when the kids piled out of the room in a cluster. Tears streamed down their young faces as their minds tried desperately to comprehend the carnage they had just witnessed. All but Timothy, who sat in his desk quietly until Mr. Richards guided him out of the room himself.

When asked if he was alright, he replied with, "I figured staying seated would be the best suitable thing to do in the situation." Mr. Richards did not reply, only delivered an odd and confused look to Timothy, who then began to smile.

Molly could not help but be distracted at work; she had more than enough building inside her tired mind. By 9am, she was ready to go home and call it a day, but Steven Wilkes MD offices sure as Hell wouldn't run itself, and she was the only receptionist on duty.

She sat in her office chair and leaned all the way back until the chair made a dangerous creak as a warning. Her thoughts went to her son, as they had been recently. She wanted to know the piece she seemed to be missing about Timothy lately. There was something extremely different about him, hidden in plain sight. It was the darkness his presence now carried. At times, when he would pass by her through the house, a pinpoint of uneasiness would slip through Molly as if her body was trying to warn her about something.

Hours passed like minutes and Molly could hear Steve approaching from the rear as he hummed loudly to himself. He had been in a jolly mood today, and frankly, it was making Molly sick.

"Hey, Molly. I need those charts for Lindsay Turner by the end of the day." He leaned in behind her, expelling his after lunch breath down the back of her neck. "She said she was shortened on her scripts and that it was my doing, that I wrote the wrong prescription. I think we may have a junkie on our hands. I want to see her file and x-ray charts once more. I need to reevaluate."

Molly could barely stand it, but smiled anyway and replied.

"Yes. Sure thing." She scooted her seat closer to her desk and further away from his breath. "I will do that as soon as I can. After lunch most likely, haven't eaten yet." She was about to go to lunch an hour ago, but demanding requests from Steve and patients set her behind. And everyone knew when Molly was hungry, Molly was irritable.

"Go ahead and take a quick lunch. Denise can handle the front for a bit." He was about to turn and walk away when he stopped himself. "Oh, and I forgot to mention. Yesterday was your fifth absence in three months. That to me is a problem."

Molly did not let him say anymore before butting in with her response.

"Sorry, Doctor Wilkes. My son's been having a rough time and it's got me sort of flustered at the moment. It is under control though. It won't happen again."

Doctor Wilkes nodded and brushed his dark hair back from his shiny forehead. His dark skin illuminated in the light. He was sweating profusely. His eyes grew large and darted behind Molly as she turned around. Molly, alarmed, whipped her head back to investigate. Nothing was there except a half empty lobby outside the waiting room glass.

"Yes, yes. I'm sure it won't." Timid and bug eyed, Steve Wilkes trotted away at a quick pace. Molly felt the goosebumps on her flesh raise, a cold sweat breaking out on her body. She looked behind her once more, only to see old lady Francine waiting at the separation glass.

"Mrs. Marrinski, your name should be called very soon. Anything I can do in the meantime?"

Francine did not reply, only gazed with a blank smile in her bulky fur coat. Her bright red lipstick shined brightly off of her crooked lips. The deep wrinkles in her face sulked downward. Her face was a mix between glum and happiness. A look she had never seen before on Francine (or Doctor Wilkes for that matter).

"Mrs. Marrinski? Everything okay?"

Francine's empty eyes slowly moved to Molly's. A small tear fell from the old woman's bright green left eye.

"He is damned now. The One has taken up quite a liking to him. It will not be long now."

Without a pause, Francine reached into her purse and brought out a small snub nosed revolver. Before Molly could grasp the situation, Francine put the gun in her mouth and pulled the trigger. The patients in the lobby screamed and darted toward the exit. The expelled brain matter reached as far as Henry Murdock, who was sitting by the two front glass double doors. Blood and chunks of brain matter landed on his jacket. He dropped the magazine he was reading and pressed himself again the large window by the doors.

Molly could not conjure up a sound. She only stood there, frozen, glaring at the blood splattered against the separation glass. Deep within her, she knew this had to be linked to the bizarre events with her son. It tickled the back of her throat with dryness, demanding to be tasted. And boy was the taste bitter. Doctor Wilkes ran from the back patient rooms with even more sweat gleaming off of his face.

"What the fuck happened?" the doctor screamed. Molly was the only one around besides the patients in the waiting room. Nurse Ramirez stood in the back hallway behind the doctor, quiet, with her arms crossed at her chest.

Molly did not have words to say. She only looked to the ground, baffled. The phone rang to her left and she answered quickly before the first ring silenced.

"Dr. Wilkes' office, how can-" She looked up at the doctor. "This is her you're speaking to-"

Doctor Wilkes moved passed her bluntly, and made his way to the waiting room to calm down the patients and check the body of the suicide victim.

The phone call was that of Principal Heyman, relaying the news of Ms. Halloway's suicide in front of the children. He asked if she could pick her son up immediately. At first, her mind could not process the events placed before her. It was like a puzzle, clear at first, before blown to bits by dynamite. Now, with only remnants of the picture left, she had to place the pieces together once again. Even if those pieces made absolutely no sense.

She told the principal she would be there as soon as she could. Doctor Wilkes however, was not so understanding.

"You're leaving now!? What am I supposed to do about these patients?"

Molly was in no mood to argue, and at this point, she barely gave a fuck about anything besides the welfare of her son.

"Someone just blew their fucking brains out in

your waiting room! After the ambulance leaves, close up!" She stormed past him and headed for the exit. Somehow, she knew things were not going to end happily for her. It was a ticking doom that she could not place and had never felt before in her entire existence. It was a feeling of lost hope, and terror.

The sun shined bright above Molly on the otherwise dark day. She reached Timothy's school in under twenty minutes as the traffic was light. They had the kids from Ms. Halloway's classroom in the counselor's room, packed tight with their faces tarnished from fear. But Timothy was in the back of the room, staring out the window. The sun silhouetted around his small frame and cast his shadow among his peers behind him. The air in the room was thick with fear and dread, yet a calm ambiance pulsated around Timothy.

Molly noticed the awkward looks from his classmates and even the principal. She was not the only one who noticed Timothy's oddly calm behavior. Principal Heyman stepped toward her quickly and guided her outside the room with his arm as he passed. Once in the hallway, he took a deep breath and smoothed his greying hair.

"She wrote 'Satin loves you' on the chalkboard in her own blood. The kids are saying she wrote it on the chalkboard with no head. Of course they have to be mistaken. That is impossible. But police are acting as if her suicide was impossible to perform. *Inhuman,* one of the officers said. I'm not sure what to believe. Hell, I'm not sure my mind has even fully grasped the situation. The only thing I can seem to think about is the fact your son wrote the same phrase over and over again on paper yesterday." His eyes turned grave. A deep, concentrated seriousness flourished upon his confused face.

Molly did not have a reply. The words SATIN LOVES YOU flashed in her mind, the same way her son wrote it. It flickered inside her head like a neon light glowing in the dark of night. No matter how hard she thought to speak, it would not come out. There was a locked door inside her and she feared it was somehow opening slowly to reveal itself – the conclusion to the growing problem.

Principal Heyman frowned at her silence. He was impatient for the outcome of his revelation to her, as if he was seeking a bit of comfort from his own agonizing dread of the unknown. Possibly, he was thinking she had answers for the questions building up inside his panicked mind. But in the end, he had nothing else to say. He blinked slowly and robotically with mental exhaustion, and walked away.

Molly stepped back inside the counselor's office and grabbed her son. Once the fresh air hit her face, for the second time in as many days, she did something she had otherwise not done in thirteen months. She lit a cigarette. She vowed to quit smoking after her father died of lung cancer, but always kept an unopened pack in her purse as a reminder of a proud victory. But today the cigarette pack was more than that. It was relief at the highest of levels. She looked down to her son, the breeze lightly lifting his brown hair as he stood focused on the sun. Molly nudged his shoulder and they both walked quickly to the car.

Another quiet night with her son, but it did not bother her as much as the last time. Molly was scared of something else she could not figure out. She slept restlessly until 3:00AM, and then strangely, she fell into a deep slumber. In the nightmare which followed, she was trapped in a dark abyss. She heard a deep voice from within the black. Somehow, she recognized the voice. It was familiar, but disguised within a husky tone.

"The tides of change are now. The transformation is unholy and pure." The voice tapered off, but the darkness drew darker. She was lost and unsure where she was. Far inside her mind, she knew it was all a dream, but that did not dampen the fear slowly filling her.

"Hello? Where am I?" Molly cried into the dark. Her voice echoed as if in some deep and hollow hallway. "What do you want with my son?" Like a key fitting perfectly into place, Molly began to understand that the dilemma revolved solely around her son. Yes, she had known this all along, only denial prevented her from fully grasping it as truth.

"The reckoning is coming forth. The damning will allow us tortured souls to once again roam free. He is the key to allow this." The voice was now deeper, like a record played in slow motion – with no echo.

In the darkness, behind even more black, Molly could barely make out a small flicker of light in front of her. She tried to walk faster but got absolutely nowhere. It made her think of how life had been recently. She could no longer get anywhere with her son. He was a closed door that was bolted shut and forbidden to be opened. The light in front of her could be the answer.

Now Molly was in a full sprint toward the glowing flicker, but the light drew further and further away until her waking eyes opened and she was once again in the darkness of her own bedroom. Her heart beat like the pounding of a steel drum. It shook her rib cage, down to her abdomen. Sweat beads dripped from her forehead and onto her pink nightgown. The room was still, quiet from everything but a low house creak toward the kitchen. The dream was not forgotten, in fact, it drowned out all her other thoughts and dominated her head.

She decided to go outside for a smoke.

The house was frozen in black and strangely quiet as she walked to the front door with the cigarette pack firm in her hand. She did not bother putting on a robe. *Fuck it, it's after 4 AM in the morning.*

The brisk morning wind collided with her warm skin, creating goosebumps on her flesh and erecting her nipples. The moon was half full and overrun with passing clouds. It was a beautiful sight to be seen. The stars shone mildly through the thick dark of the sky. Molly's head was frozen upward, amazed at the portrait laid in front of her. Below her peripherals, her dead husband walked clumsily to the front deck. His walk was inhuman but did not make a sound. His kneecaps repeatedly snapped inward and outward silently with each step. Molly spotted him at the foot of the steps. She stifled a scream inside her mouth and stepped backward in shock.

"Hey hunny bunny, need to make a pit stop." He giggled at his remark and began up the steps. His clothes were ripped and dirtied along with his skin. He was wearing the suit he had been buried in. His short hair stuck to his mud engulfed cranium and his eyes sunk deep inside his head. He looked as if he had just escaped from his own watery grave.

Molly continued to scream underneath her tightened hand. Timothy's deceased father smiled at her shock, sniffed her hair briefly, and walked around her inside the house. Molly could not move; her feet were cemented to the ground. Fear was an understatement, her body vibrated from it. She turned her head and saw he was walking upstairs to Timothy's room. Her feet disconnected simultaneously and she fell to the floor, trying to walk. She quickly got up and headed to the foot of the stairs. He was gone and out of sight.

Molly made her way up the stairs slowly, her head frozen forward. She knew he would be in Timothy's room. And he was, staring down at his son like the proud father he could have been if he hadn't taken his own life.

"When he was a kid, I knew he was destined for greatness. But I never imagined this." His dead eyes lit up with joy. Molly could see the lacerations around his neck from the rope under the smeared dirt. "Our son is their only hope for Hell."

Molly stepped back. Both her son and his father's face were now dark red with rubber like scales. Small horns protruded from their hairlines and their glossy black eyes showed Molly only fire. Timothy sat up and smiled at his father.

Molly woke up back in her bed, surrounded by damp sheets. She had been crying in her sleep. Above her, in her son's room, she heard the cracking of floor boards. Immediately, Molly dashed out of bed and made for Timothy's bedroom. He was grinning in the darkness, propped up against his headboard.

"I can't sleep, mom. Haven't been able to sleep well." The grin did not leave, which creeped Molly out to the fullest. But the fact he had engaged in conversation with her, was relief all in its own.

"Why can't you sleep, hon?" She was genuinely concerned, but her voice was still shaken from the dreams; it came out rushed and forced.

"Because it's almost time, I think. They are all making sure everything is going as planned." With this, he slumped back into his bed and closed his eyes as his mother's chest sank to her stomach from the reply.

Molly's reaction was silence, and after five

minutes of gazing at her now sleeping son, she went back downstairs to her room.

Molly's life was falling apart piece by piece, and she did not even understand the reasoning as of why. It just was, and that was all she had to go on. Sometimes, life's biggest predicaments are the ones that remain unseen. Only, Molly was now realizing this was no ordinary life predicament. This was something far more sinister. It was a storm from which there was no shelter.

Molly fell asleep to the memories of her husband up to the suicide, where he hung himself in the garage on Christmas Eve. She noticed a change in his behavior weeks prior to his death, but never did she think he would take his own life. Timothy was two years old, and the loss affected him mildly when Molly told him his father would not be coming back.

The reason why he did it was not a global mystery, as his life was no royal bliss. The alcoholism was a problem that grew in magnitude every year until he was polishing off more than a fifth of liquor and a six pack of beer a night. It was his presence she felt in the dream, she knew that much for sure. The mystery was more so if it was actually a dream or not.

All of this did not add up to anything. It only shrouded more darkness upon the truth. The last thoughts of the night were the lips of her dead husband, stretched morbidly into that grin which haunted her. She remembered that grin all too well.

The next morning, the sun shined bright as if to tell Molly everything was going to be alright. But Molly did not feel alright, and Timothy was unusually happy. Seeing Timothy happy was usually a good thing to Molly, but the extent of his happiness had a sinister appeal to it she did not like. She decided to keep him home from school, she couldn't stomach another incident.

"What would you like for breakfast, cereal?" She wanted to match her son's joy, only her mentality would not allow it. She felt broken and scared for what the day might bring her. Timothy looked up briefly from the kitchen table and nodded his head with a smile.

Molly went to the cupboard, grabbed a box of Krunchies and poured it into a bowl. She pictured Tim's dead father sitting next to him at the table, waiting for breakfast too with a deep laceration around his broken neck. He sported the same grin as the night before. Wildly, she could see Timothy was acting as if someone was next to him; his eyes kept meeting his dead father's. It began to crawl all over Molly's skin until her heart was leaping out of her chest.

"What do you keep looking at?!" Molly snapped as she flung herself around to face her son.

Timothy only giggled and shook his head. There was something different about his eyes that Molly couldn't put a finger on; something primal and out of place.

Finally, he spoke.

"What ever is the problem, Mother?" He sounded fake, like a child from a 1950's family sitcom. But his eyes told a completely different story. She could swear the blackness of his pupils was spreading. It gave out an inhuman gaze.

Molly turned back around and poured milk into the cereal bowl.

"Nothing. Long night I guess." She was too scared to belt out the truth at this monster that now inhabited her son. She was fearful to even be in the same vicinity.

As the milk splashed through the cereal, filling up the bowl to a reasonable amount, Molly heard a low growl behind her. She froze up, her breath stopped in mid exhale, and her eyes dried up inside her head. She could not move, and the milk overflowed the top of the bowl, spread across the counter, and spilled to the floor. A warm breath hit the back of her neck, fluttering the remaining pieces of hair that did not make it into the ponytail.

Molly whipped around, flinging the bowl of Krunchies off to the linoleum. The glass bowl crashed and shattered, sending milk and cereal across the light blue floor. Timothy was sitting where he had been, and even though she felt the air on her neck, it could not have been her son. Although, the smirk on his face said otherwise.

"Wow, Mother. You must be so stressed. Let me clean this all up for you." Timothy stood from his chair with his face barely changing expressions. He was like a control panel for something much more powerful and ancient.

"No! Stay there! I got-" Molly caught herself from the sudden outburst. Unexpected tears dropped from the rims of her eyes. "Please, just go up to your room for a little while."

Timothy hummed to himself while walking up the stairs to his room. Once at the top, he turned to his mother who was watching him at the foot of the steps.

"There's nothing to be afraid of, Mother. Everything will soon be set right."

And then, he was gone.

Molly rushed for the kitchen – more accurately, the cabinet above the stove. She downed three swigs of whiskey from the bottle before pouring it into a small glass. It would take a lot of alcohol for her to catch her breath. She pictured Timothy's teacher walking over to the chalkboard headless, but with much intent still left in her. SATAN LOVES YOU. Those words dominated her now. It was a small glimpse into a future that may yet exist.

Why was she so fearful of her own son? And why did he not feel like her son anymore? Molly finished the whiskey in the glass and sat it on the table. Before she knew it, she was falling asleep at the kitchen table while keeping an eye on the stairs for Timothy to descend.

Now, midday came upon her and Timothy still remained unseen, barricaded inside his bedroom. Molly went in and out of mini naps, flicking through the channels on the television with one leg propped up on the couch. She didn't remember the last time she was able to relax – sure, Doctor Heyman called twice and Molly didn't dare answer, but she wrote it off as somewhat entitlement. In her mind, she had earned this. Her son was driving her absolutely insane, and if having a couple drinks morning to midday while sprawled on the couch was somehow wrong, well so fucking be it.

Timothy barely had any control over his own hand. It gripped the pencil tight as it whipped around the white paper, sketching a portrait of primal beauty. Tears of happiness streamed from his eyes as he made out his sketch. His hand twitched back and forth as he shaded in the long and broad horns above His head. It was a masterpiece. It was the final clue to finish the long awaited puzzle. Timothy held the picture of Him up to the light. The gleam of the sun rays somehow darkened the picture.

"It is time, Tim." The voice came from behind him like a cold breeze.

He whirled around to see the man in his drawing come to life. Only, it was no man. It was his own personal savior of darkness.

The savior opened up his arms wide and waited for Timothy's embrace, which came soon after.

Molly packed the laundry basket full of dirty clothes piled in her bedroom corner. It was a long time coming, and it was finally fucking time to get some of this goddam laundry done. Once full, she breathed an annoyed sigh and made her way to the basement where the appliances resided.

The basement was cold and always carried an abnormally loud echo, but today it seemed extra creepy. It felt like a dungeon, a place of torment and fear. She half expected to see her dead husband again, in the corner, waiting for her arrival. But the room was empty, and the only sound audible was the slow trickle of water from a leaky pipe above.

As she unloaded the clothes and stuffed them

into the washer, she did not hear or acknowledge the small footsteps descending the stairs behind her until it was too late. As Molly turned back to see her son, her mind completely erased sanity or any chance of reaction. Her son's eyes were removed and replaced with black and bloody holes of nothing. His lips were dried and cracked, and he resembled more of a fifty-year-old man than a twelve-year-old boy. He wielded a butcher knife, held tight between his little fingers.

Before Molly could even gasp, Timothy swung the knife at his mother's throat, cutting her head almost clean off. She choked and sprayed blood back at him, which splattered on his smiling face. She tumbled backward to the cold concrete, and propped against the dryer, partially reconnecting her severed head.

Timothy could hear applause all around him; it was a victory of the greatest of power. He had finally set forth the path that was awaiting him all along. The Savior appeared once again in front of him as the ground around them began to crumble, spewing light from flames that surrounded them. The heat from below scorched Timothy's skin with a rejuvenating sense of renewal. The Beast held out his gargantuan clawed hands and waited for Timothy. He placed his small hand in His, and together, they descended into their kingdom.

"Remember, I love you Timothy."

# ABOUT THE ARTIST

Josh Davis is an American author from Flint, Michigan. Josh began writing articles for various horror sites before landing a place in Rejected for Content 4: Highway to Hell with his gripping tale of cannibalism 'Confession of Mortal Sins'. Since then he has appeared in several JEA published anthologies such as Triggered and Full Moon Slaughter 2: Altered Beasts. He is working on another collection as well as a novel and resides in Montrose, Michigan with his fiance Pebbles Keith who also writes short stories in the horror genre.

Josh enjoys spending time with his three kids

Selena, Lydia, and Linkin, and making a name for himself in the horror industry. Stay tuned....

Made in the USA
Middletown, DE
21 October 2018